Praise

EVEN DEAD MEN

"A true *whodunit* filled with suspense, chess trivia and entertaining characters."
- Idaho Statesman

"I loved the plot, became highly attached to the characters and enjoyed learning a bit about chess all at the same time."
- Long and Short Reviews

"...be prepared to read it at one go, because once you pick it up you don't feel like (putting) it down unless you are done with it." *- Indian Book Reviews*

"If you are looking for something new and fresh in the crime genre, look no further. I enjoyed this book from page one."
- Carey O., Amazon customer

"I loved the book and fell right into it from the first few sentences."
- Julie's Book Reviews

"...one of the most amazing stories I have ever read."
- Goodreads review

Other Books by
Michael Weitz

The Grandmaster's King
Till Tomorrow

www.michael-weitz.com

EVEN DEAD MEN PLAY CHESS

MICHAEL WEITZ

Black Fence Books

Even Dead Men Play Chess
By Michael Weitz
Copyright © Michael Weitz, 2015

...

...

This book is a work of fiction. While references may be made to actual places or events, the names, characters, incidents, and locations within are from the author's imagination and are not a resemblance to actual living or dead persons, businesses, or events. Any similarity is coincidental.

...

First published by Lachesis Publishing, March 2009
Published by Musa Publishing, August 2012
Published by Black Fence Books, April 2015

...

ISBN: 978-0692430613

Published in the United States of America
Editor: JoAnne Soper-Cook

For Catherine,
my wife, my partner, my friend

1

Erica Minor died on her seventh birthday. She had been small for her age, tied pink ribbons in her hair, wore second-hand dresses to school, and though quiet, was not as shy as her teachers thought. More than anything, she had wanted to keep her home life a secret.

When the story of Erica's death appeared in the newspapers the next day, the public was outraged. There were interviews with city officials on morning radio and TV programs, newspaper headlines, and heated op-ed pieces for days. But it was all too late. Erica had needed help long before she died.

Donald and Judy Minor, Erica's parents, were meth-heads. They made, sold, and used methamphetamine, a drug so dangerous that almost every first-time user becomes addicted to it.

The kitchen in Erica's house looked more like a chemistry lab than an area where a family stored food and prepared meals. It was cluttered with stained glass tubes, jars, and bottles. Copper pipe twisted and turned, connecting one container to another. Propane tanks stood like squat sentinels in the corners, and it was littered everywhere with small, white cardboard boxes and the ravaged foil blister packs of cold and allergy medications.

At two in the afternoon, while her parents were at the kitchen counter crystallizing a fresh batch of the drug, Erica crawled along the floor, quietly searching through drawers and cabinets until she finally found a butane barbeque lighter to ignite her birthday candles with.

Donald and Judy left the kitchen when a customer knocked on their front door. They never even knew their daughter had been in the room with them. The coroner said Erica's death was due to severe internal injuries and the third degree burns she'd suffered after she had lit the candles on her birthday cake, igniting the combustible noxious fumes in the room and causing her house to explode.

Erica's ten-year old brother, Jason, told all of this to me from his hospital bed. He'd pressed himself to the floor beneath the dining room table and watched it all until he was mercifully knocked unconscious by the blast. But he'd seen his baby sister thrown against the kitchen ceiling and swallowed by flames before he passed out.

Jason and I talked a lot, but never about anything as horrific as watching your baby sister die. Usually we discussed video games, television shows, and fast food restaurants. My name is Ray Gordon. I'm a chess teacher.

I was thinking about my talks with Jason while I stood within the Lake View Cemetery, dressed in a black suit, surrounded by a crowd of a hundred people. I didn't know most of them, but the gathering was lightly salted with a handful of recognizable faces from the youth center where I taught most of my students. Jason Minor was up front, near the casket and beneath a green canvas canopy. He sat next to a woman who must have been his grandmother, judging by her steely gray hair and the giant orchid pinned above her left breast.

Donald and Judy Minor weren't present at their daughter's funeral. They were handcuffed to their respective hospital beds, recovering from superficial wounds sustained in the explosion. The usually emotionless local TV news reporters shook their heads sadly at the camera after Judy Minor offered only a blank expression through her stringy hair when asked about the death of her daughter. Doctors showed the TV audience colorful computer-generated images that compared a healthy human brain to a spongy-looking brain affected by methamphetamine.

One doctor went so far as to say Judy Minor had been using meth so long her brain looked like a lump of Swiss cheese left out in the sun. Her daughter's death probably only registered as a minor nuisance.

It was a nice day for a funeral, bright and crisp with the kind of blue sky I wished I could dive into and discover what lay behind the clouds. The air was cool, and many of the attendees wore coats or sweaters. But by noon the sun seemed to win the push/pull between summer and autumn. It was the kind of day my parents were buried on. A good day for a hike in the mountains.

My reverie was shattered by a group of angry people who marched on the sidewalk outside the cemetery. They carried cardboard signs that read *Meth Kills* and chanted,

"The Minors murdered her with meth!" I only hoped Jason wasn't paying attention to all the hype surrounding his baby sister's death.

My wristwatch beeped, and I muffled it with my hand before pushing the tiny button to silence the alarm. Several people turned and glared as if I'd just spit. It wasn't like I had answered my cell phone! Nevertheless, the alarm on my watch triggered a chain reaction of heads tilting toward their own timepieces. Nobody wanted to be there. No matter how nice a day it was or how much time they could get off of work. Not one person wanted to be at the funeral for a seven-year-old girl.

I got home from the funeral an hour later than I'd hoped I would. It was just before three p.m. and I had an appointment at six. Normally not a problem, but between where I was and where I had to be was a two-and-a-half hour drive. I still needed to get my mail out and finish packing.

I ran to the window and looked up the street. The mailman was four houses up, his glorified ice cream truck parked at the curb while he delivered a package. I dashed back to my table where a postcard had waited for two days. It was already addressed and contained some arcane scribbles on the back, notation recognized only by chess players, but it wasn't ready to go out just yet.

I looked out the window again, and then at the chessboard in front of me. I stared at the page of notes I'd made over the week and then wrote *23. Rad1* on the postcard. It was my next move in a chess game being played through the U.S. Postal Service.

When I opened my front door, the little white truck chugged in front of my neighbor's house while the mailman stuffed letters and magazines into the mailbox at the curb. I walked slowly until the postman gave his rig a little gas, and then adjusted my gait to arrive with him at my mailbox.

"I didn't realize what time it was," I said, walking up to the truck.

"Another game, Ray?" he said when I handed him the postcard.

"I'm in a correspondence tournament." I nodded. "I've got that along with my regular games."

"How many is that?"

I had to think for a moment. "Twenty-three."

"Jeez! That's a lot of postage. How long does it take to play a game of chess by mail? I always see these cards from you and for you."

"Years." I bounced on my toes with pride. Chess was fun no matter how I played, from five-minute speed games to contests spanning address changes and multiple birthday parties.

"Why not use the Internet? Wouldn't e-mail be cheaper?"

"This coming from a postman?" I laughed, then shrugged. "Some people do use e-mail, but this is more traditional. In fact," I said with an I'm-so-smart bounce of my heels, "the first Correspondence Chess Champion of the World, an Australian guy named Purdy, said correspondence chess is the purest form of the game. There are no distractions, no clocks—just chess. Even e-mail is too fast. If both players are sitting at their computers at the same time, they end up just playing the whole game. Or they blunder moves, because of the distraction of the other player waiting. Besides, it's fun to get mail."

"You're nuts." The mailman handed me a stack of what looked like nothing but junk.

"I know. Certifiable." I smiled and gave him a quick salute. For a correspondence chess player, I was considered only mildly insane for juggling twenty-three games. Two of my opponents conducted sixty or more chess games by mail.

I trudged back up the sidewalk and shuffled through the envelopes. There were two postcards addressed to me with similar notations to the one I'd just sent. I put those next to my chessboard and dropped the rest of the stack on my desk to look over later.

"Morphy!" I called. "Get your leash."

Morphy was my four-year-old mutt, part yellow lab and part "other big dog," and he was my best friend. He bounced into my bedroom with his leash hanging limp between his jaws like a fresh kill.

My duffle bag had been mostly packed before I'd left for the funeral, so I just tossed in a small bag of overnight toiletries and an extra shirt. In the living room, I stuffed a small binder with all twenty-three of my correspondence chess games (including the two moves I'd just received) into the duffle bag, then grabbed a chess book about tactics. I rifled through it until I found the game I wanted, added it to the bag, and zipped it up.

At three ten, the lights were off, drapes drawn, porch light on, and the dog leapt in anticipation. I grabbed a handful of CDs, and Morphy and I were out the door. It would be close. Just getting out of Seattle would take a half hour to forty-five minutes.

For the past five years, I'd been volunteering at the Brookstone Youth Center. I didn't have a degree in psychology or sociology, but I did what I could. I am a chess nut, and I taught the kids chess. Maybe Jason Minor talked to me about his sister because I was not an official counselor or maybe because we had chess in common.

Once I reached Master level, I began getting requests to teach adults some of the finer nuances of the game. I took on a few students outside of the youth center, mostly men in their thirties or forties who were looking to improve their club play. I'd go to their homes or we'd meet somewhere on the University of Washington campus.

When I'd received a call from Walter Kelly, one hundred fifty miles away in Yakima, asking me to help him figure out why he was losing such a high percentage of his over-the-board battles, I'd turned him down flat. I hadn't wanted to spend that much time on the road. Besides, there were plenty of players in Yakima better than me. "Doesn't matter," he'd said. "I think we can help each other."

"What do you mean?" I'd asked.

"I knew your mother."

My parents died when I was eleven years old. They were caught between a drunk driver and an eighteen-wheeler. So when Walter Kelly had said he had known my mom, two and a half hours of drive time didn't seem very long at all. Once a month, sometimes more, when our schedules meshed, I'd drive to Yakima to dispense any chessic wisdom I could, and then listened to tales of my mother in her youth over dinner.

Walter couldn't come to Seattle because he took care of his wife, Margie. Years earlier, she'd suffered a cracked vertebra when she fell from a ladder at work. Her employer and six doctors had agreed her injury was severe and warranted surgery, but the bureaucrats at Labor and Industries had refused to okay any operation until *they* were satisfied it was absolutely necessary.

When she could no longer stand up straight, one of those doctors had performed the surgical procedure Margie had needed a year and a half earlier, and logged it as part of a liposuction for a different patient.

For the better part of a year, I got to know my mother in a way I may never have, even if she had lived. She and Walt had dated in high school. He was two years her senior, and the romance didn't last, but he was still able to tell me how she'd revved the engine of her father's Chevy and then jammed the shifter into drive. She'd done it in front of the high school the day after getting her driver's license, which meant all of her friends were able to witness the drive shaft succumb to the sudden force of the engine and explode off of the axle. I wondered if my mother would have told me that story had she been alive when I turned sixteen.

Walter showed me the two high school yearbooks he had with her pictures, along with photos from their prom. The first time I brought Morphy with me, Walt told me about the dog my mother had owned since she was ten. It was a beagle named Rudy, and when he got killed by a delivery truck, she'd cried every day for a month. So I learned that my mother was where my love for my own dog came from. I teared up just thinking about when Morphy would be gone.

At Ellensburg, I eased into the right hand lane of the freeway and headed south on I-82.

It's a half-hour drive between Ellensburg, home of Central Washington University and Yakima, the "Palm Springs of Washington."

The citizens of Yakima were pretty much divided over that particular moniker as a nickname for a city usually known for apples, but either way, the sign was there for all to see.

Just before getting into Yakima, I turned west on the freeway, then got off on the 16th Avenue exit. Like almost every city in the country, Yakima has its roster of streets named for trees, and as I turned up Chestnut Avenue, I was met by towering oaks, elms, and willows, all brandishing their fall foliage. The reds, oranges, and yellows popped against the deep blue October sky like an artist's canvas. *Good work, God*, I thought.

Morphy whined and cried when I turned into the Kellys' driveway. He either needed to seriously take a leak or was anxious to see Walt and Margie. Probably a little of both.

I got out and stretched while Morphy sniffed the hedge line and lifted his leg against the telephone pole by the sidewalk.

We were fifteen minutes late. Usually, I was on time for everything I did. My uncle Dave, who raised me after my parents were killed, had little toleration for people who couldn't keep track of their own lives. "Sometimes things happen to mess up your day," he'd say, "but not nearly as often as people simply not keeping track of the time. It's just a matter of planning. Never be too lazy to plan, Ray."

I knocked on the front door knowing Walt would grill me about being late. Luckily, Morphy was my pal, and he was cute and happy and begged for everyone's attention, so Walt would only have a minute or two to dish it out.

But when the door opened, it wasn't Walt standing in front of me. Instead, it was his son, Brian Kelly. Brian and I were close in age. I guessed he was a year or two older than me and he had me beat in the weight department by at least twenty pounds. He was six foot three and had hair the color of sawdust.

Brian had been the star quarterback on his high school football team and gone to Washington State University with high expectations. The college life got the better of him, though, and Brian missed too many practices and too many classes. His grades sagged, and eventually, he was no longer an athlete. He'd messed up his chance and by the time he'd figured it out, it was too late. But he'd stayed in school, then came home to Yakima, and was one of the best veterinarians in town, according to Walt.

Brian let me in and watched Morphy go unabashedly off on his own. "With everything that's happened, Mom must have forgotten you were coming," he said.

"What do you mean? What's happened? The police finally hear about me?" Brian didn't return my smile, so I let mine drop. "What's wrong?"

"Ray, my dad's dead."

2

■ "What?" I said. "I didn't know he was sick. My God, Brian, what happened? When?"

"Why don't you come in and talk to Mom. She'd like some company."

Margie was in the living room, sitting in an old La-Z-Boy, with Morphy's chin in her lap. "Hello, Raymond," she said when I entered the room.

"Hi, Margie. Here, let me keep Morph from bothering you."

"You'll do no such thing. He's doing what he senses he should do, and I'm inclined to believe he's doing me some good. Look how quiet and gentle he's being. He knows something is wrong."

I sat down on the edge of the sofa and heard Brian rummaging in the kitchen. The La-Z-Boy Margie sat in, another chair, and the sofa all had hand-made afghans draped over their backs. Margie had taken up crocheting when her back kept her from working and had made dozens for family and friends. They were chevron-patterned, with rich blues and deep crimsons bordering seas of creamy white.

It was quiet. Whenever I'd been there in the past, music floated through the house, or maybe the nightly news was on the television. With Walter gone, there was just silence, except for a clock ticking from somewhere down the hallway. It felt like the staccato beat struggled to be heard through the heavy air. Perhaps even the clock was trying to be quiet, respectfully ticking its tocks without causing too much annoyance.

"Can I ask you what happened, Margie?" I asked.

She stared at a spot somewhere in front of my feet while her hand slowly stroked the top of Morphy's head. I wasn't sure if she'd heard me. Maybe she wasn't ready to talk about the death of her husband. I listened to the faraway clock, and had just decided to join Brian in the kitchen, when her gaze lifted up to mine.

"I found him at lunch time on Saturday. Out in his shop. He must have slipped, or tripped or something. I don't know."

"Was it a heart attack?" I asked.

Margie's eyes flooded over, and she slowly shook her head. "No. At least I don't think so. He...he fell on one of his saws. I can't bear the thought of it. There was so much blood! I'm sorry, Raymond. I can't..."

"It's okay, Margie. I didn't mean to make you upset. Can I get you anything?"

She shook her head. "Brian's already making us some tea."

Right on cue, Brian came into the living room carrying a tray laden with cups, saucers, a fat porcelain teapot, and a variety of sweeteners. He was dressed in black slacks and a white shirt with the sleeves rolled up to his elbows. A small kitchen towel was draped over his right forearm, giving the impression of an off-duty butler making one more call for the mistress of the house.

He set the tray on the coffee table without rattling the dishes, then scooped a spoon of sugar into a delicate cup and poured some tea for his mother. Margie watched the ritual intently, her gaze never leaving Brian's hands. When he handed her the cup and saucer, she held it on her lap with one hand and returned the other to Morphy's head.

"Ray?" Brian asked.

"Please." Being from Seattle, I'm strictly a coffee man, but I didn't think it was the right time to be picky.

When the three of us each had our tea and sat back in the stillness, I looked at Brian and then at Margie. Brian shrugged.

"Where were you when this happened?" I asked him.

"At the clinic. We're open until noon on Saturdays. Mom called right before we closed up."

"I don't know how long he was like that," Margie said. "If I'd gone out sooner, maybe I could have done something."

To say Walt Kelly had been something of a woodworker would be to say retired world champion Garry Kasparov was something of a chess player. Walt had been featured in a few carpentry enthusiast magazines, and was considered by his colleagues to be an artist more than just a weekend hobbyist. Nothing seemed to be beyond his skills. He had built all of the kitchen cabinetry, the dining room set, the deck furniture, and a grandfather clock for his and Margie's home. His grandkids received rocking horses in the shapes of gorillas, fish, giraffes — anything but a horse.

When Walt had insisted on paying me for chess lessons, I'd asked to be paid with a chessboard. His reply had been a smile.

"I felt helpless," Margie said into her teacup. "With my back the way it is, I couldn't even..."

"It's okay, Mom," Brian said. "You don't have to keep putting yourself through this. There was nothing anybody could have done."

Walt had taken me out to his shop several times, and while I'm no expert, it was easy to see how Walt's set-up would make any woodworking aficionado drool. The shop itself was large enough to house three cars comfortably, even with the workbench that spanned one wall. It had been a few months since I'd seen it, but I remembered saws of all kinds, from handsaws to powered miter saws, and I had a hard time picturing how Walt must have died.

"Ray, would you give me a hand in the kitchen?" Brian asked. It was as if he sensed the question forming on my tongue.

I refilled Margie's cup and took the teapot into the kitchen. "What's up?" I asked.

"The look on your face. I just didn't want to make Mom relive it again."

"Sorry. Was I that obvious?"

"Getting there. It's okay. It looks like Dad was up on a stool getting a piece of wood out of the rack and fell. He landed on the table saw."

"But how could that really do anything? It might have gouged him, but…"

"It was on," Brian said.

"What? Your dad was climbing around above a running table saw? That doesn't sound like him."

"Not normally, but I've seen him do things like that before. He'd let the band saw go or leave the table saw on if it was just going to be a second while he got another piece of wood or something."

Walt Kelly had been working wood since before taking high school shop. Though he hadn't owned or used every power tool out there, he'd either read about it, borrowed it, or seen it demonstrated at a trade show. He'd built hundreds of picture frames, tables, benches, boxes, chairs, chests, stools, shelves, and who knew what else. Yet the last time I'd seen him, he still had ten fingers. I assumed he had all of his toes, too.

I knew he'd been careful when he worked out in the shop. On the bench by the door was a tray where he and visitors put watches, rings, and other jewelry. He never wore long sleeves or loose shirts, either. Margie would cut the arms off of anything to be worn in the shop and then sew up the frayed ends. How could Walt Kelly have been so careful his whole life, so conscientious of what could happen, and then leave a table saw running while standing above it on a stool?

"What did the police say?" I asked.

Brian shrugged as he cleaned out the tea strainer. "It's pretty obvious he fell. There was a stool on the floor and a stick of wood hanging down from the storage rack. I wonder if he had a heart attack, though." He shrugged again, and scooped some fresh black tea into the strainer.

"How was his health?"

"I don't know. Dad never really discussed that kind of stuff. I don't even know if Mom knew."

"Of course I knew."

Brian and I looked up. Margie stood in the doorway of the kitchen.

3

■ In the short time I'd known him, Walter Kelly had seemed healthy enough for a man his age. It was for his sixtieth birthday he'd originally called me. Having loved chess his entire life but never having achieved a high rating, he'd thought lessons were just the thing to give himself as a birthday gift. Far from being the type to jump out of a cake, I'd never been a birthday present. But it had seemed like a good idea after he told me about his short, teenaged romance with my mother.

Walter had never let on about any health problems of his own. He'd always said that Margie, who at that time was still four years away from the big six-oh, had enough problems to keep them and their insurance company busy.

"Your father was fine," Margie told her son. We'd migrated from the quietly comfortable living room to the kitchen, where more hot water stirred within the bowels of the teakettle on the stove. "As a matter of fact, he'd just had a check-up last month."

Brian nodded to himself and turned his attention to the teapot. "All right, Mom." Just then the kettle shrieked, putting an exclamation point on the end of the discussion.

"So…when's the funeral?" I asked.

"Tomorrow." Brian turned away and poured the hot water into the pot.

I glanced at my watch. "Well, I suppose I'll head back to Seattle then. I didn't bring a suit, but I can be back first thing in the morning."

"Oh, Ray, you don't need to do that. Brian has a suit you can borrow. Why don't you and Morphy stay here tonight, and let Brian go home to Julie," Margie said.

I'd seen photos of Brian's wife on the obligatory "wall-o'-pictures" in the Kelly household, but I'd never met her. I had been informed at some point that Julie was a pharmacist at a grocery store.

Brian looked at me like I was his all-time favorite baseball hero and he'd just asked for an autograph. I was getting puppy dog eyes from him *and* Morphy.

Margie saw me waver and offered to order a pizza. "I just haven't felt like cooking," she explained.

Her husband had just died and I was thinking only of myself. "Of course I'll stay, Margie. Thank you."

Brian eased out a long sigh. *Thank you*, he mouthed at me. "I know just the suit," he said. "I'll bring it by later."

I nodded. "One question. Who's got the best pizza in town?" Brian and Margie remained silent. "Does that mean nobody, or that there's a family disagreement?"

Brian smiled and pushed himself away from the counter. "I'm going to go take Julie out for Mexican before she starts to make hot dogs or something."

When Brian was gone, Margie returned to the kitchen and fixed herself another cup of tea. She stirred in two spoons of honey and added a squirt of lemon juice from the fridge. After a testing sip, she scanned a list of phone numbers by the telephone, then called in an order for a large pizza with pepperoni and black olives. Somehow Margie remembered my favorite toppings — which happened to have been my dad's, as well. "Come and join me in the living room, Raymond. It's much more comfortable in there."

Margie returned to the old chair she'd sat in when I arrived, and Morphy took up his position at her side, where she could easily pat his head. I sat across from her on the sofa and listened to the clock tick from down the hall for a few minutes.

"You know Brian and Walter never really saw eye to eye on things," Margie finally said.

"Like what?"

"Oh, lots of things. You for one."

"Me?"

Margie smiled thinly. "Well, not you as much as what you represent. Brian thought Walter wasted too much time and money on chess."

First of all, no one can waste too much time or money on chess.

Second of all, I'd seen Walter's collection of chess paraphernalia. He had a few books about tactics and a couple of general volumes about the overall game. He had two sets of pieces: one nice wooden one for home, and a plastic set to take to tournaments and his chess club. Walter Kelly was way below average when it came to chess obsession. The president of my chess club in Seattle owned thirty-six different sets of pieces, five clocks, twenty-two boards, and six hundred seventy-two books about chess. And he was sane.

There are more books written about chess than all of the other games and sports combined. A handful of reading material about the royal game was certainly not going overboard.

"What about the woodworking?" I asked. If there was a woodworker's club, Walter would have been president, no question.

"Brian grew up around that. He never quite embraced it the way Walter hoped he might, but I don't think Brian approved of that, either."

"Why not?"

"He never really put much stock into hobbies. He was always about his sports."

"Was it a problem between them?"

"Not really. We always supported Brian. He just has a different outlook on life. It's just too bad they didn't get a chance to resolve their differences."

"Walt never told me they were having trouble," I said.

Margie shook her head. "I don't expect he would have. Walt and I are both proud of Brian. We've never seen any reason to air family disagreements."

"I can understand that," I said.

But there was something more. Margie looked at Morphy, sipped tea, and then threw a shy glance my way. She'd wanted me to stay and Brian, her son, to leave. The chitchat had to lead somewhere. "Margie," I said quietly, "what do you really want to talk about? What don't you want Brian to know?"

She set her teacup on the coffee table and sat back with her hands clasped in her lap. "I've never been any good at hiding my feelings. When Brian broke his ankle in junior high, I cried and acted like he'd contracted some terminal disease. I was so scared. When I found out about my back, I tried to be brave, but—"

"Margie," I interrupted.

She sighed. "On Friday night, Walter was acting very peculiar."

"In what way?"

"He was nervous. I think he was scared of something or someone. When I asked what was going on, he said he needed to go to the library to look up something about his new project out in the shop."

"Did he leave?"

Margie nodded quickly. "He was gone for two hours. When he came home, he seemed mad."

"Because of what he found at the library?"

"Ray. You've seen all the books he has on wood and tools and projects and all those things. Anybody who needs a book about woodworking comes here, not the public library."

"Why would he lie to you?"

"I don't know," she whispered, her eyes pleading.

"Did you tell the police about it?"

She looked at Morphy and scratched his ears. "No. It didn't seem important, and I suppose it doesn't make any difference now."

I took a sip of my tea and remembered my own incident, which had involved Walter but didn't seem to make any difference now. He'd called and left me a voicemail on Friday night. "Ray, I've got a big problem with the Evergreen Game," he'd said. "I'll see you later." That was it. Walt had never been real verbose on the phone, so I hadn't bothered to call him back. I'd known what he meant.

In 1852, a chess game was played between two Germans, Adolf Anderssen and Jean Dufresne, in Berlin and became known as the Evergreen Game. Wilhelm Steinitz, who later became the first World Chess Champion, dubbed the game "Evergreen" because the ideas behind Anderssen's brilliant moves and tactical displays would remain fresh and exciting to generations of chess players to follow.

Anderssen put on a stunning show of piece sacrifices, ending up without a Queen and Rook, against his opponent's positional play that allowed Anderssen's sacrifices and perhaps even gave him a cavalier attitude toward the game. In the end, Steinitz was right. Hundreds of chess books over the years had analyzed the positions, teachers still embedded the ideas into their students' chessic memories, and the Anderssen/Dufresne Evergreen Game of 1852 lived on.

After Erica's funeral, I'd found one of my chess books with a move-by-move analysis of the game and had brought it with me to discuss with Walt.

I wondered if Margie could have misunderstood Walt when he'd said he was going to the library to find help for a woodworking project. Maybe he'd gone for chess books. I didn't get a chance to ask, though, because the doorbell rang.

4

■ I'd heard once when I was in college that pizza was like sex. Even bad pizza was still pretty good pizza. Nevertheless, by the time we were finished with dinner and Morphy had licked the grease from the empty pizza box, I was still unsure if Margie and her son disagreed on who had the best pizza in town, or if they were all bad.

Margie and I watched *Jeopardy!* without any further discussion about Walter. She had a third cup of tea during the show and then called it a night.

"I hope you'll forgive my poor manners, Raymond. I haven't been sleeping well. In fact, I've been using a little help. And I need to take it now."

"Of course, Margie. Don't worry about it."

"You can sleep in the guest bedroom. Do you remember where it is?"

I nodded. "Do you mind if I look around a bit?"

"You make yourself right at home. Good night."

"Good night, Margie."

It was just past eight p.m. on a crisp October night. What little light was left in the sky breathed its last wispy rays, and the streetlights had already come on to cast pale white iridescence on the pavement.

Two doors down the hallway on the right was Walt's den. I poked my head in and flipped on the lights. This was where Walt and I would go through my lessons and replay famous chess games. Two walls were adorned with built-in shelves dedicated to Walt's woodworking book collection. There were hardcover books concerning household projects and repair; thinner volumes about building furniture (both indoor and out); manuals about the use and care of power tools; books about wood stains and finishes; books about glues, caulks, and other adhesives; even a few titles about which screws to use with what species of wood. There were five gray binders, neatly organized by year, with purchase and warranty information of tools, appliances, and other household items, and a shelf of thin boxes containing old issues of three different magazines about carpentry.

A desk at the far end of the room was littered with graph paper, rulers, pencils, and protractors. Closest to the door on a short wall was the chess table, with the board and pieces set up, ready for battle.

I turned off the lights, stepped back into the hallway, and shut the door to the room.

At the front door, I played with the lock until I was confident I wouldn't have to wake Margie in order to let me back in, then I took Morphy outside to get my duffel bag from the Land Cruiser.

Before I got to my car, I looked to my right and saw Walt's darkened shop. It was an extension of the garage that invaded the backyard like a landslide. It wasn't gaudy or out of place because Margie had insisted on keeping it in context with their home. There was no way she would have allowed him to erect a great tin box of a shed. Nor had Walter wanted to. After all, it had given him the opportunity to do more of what he loved — build.

Once the shop had been built to Walt's needs and wants, they'd picked new colors for their home. A grayish blue, the color of warm steel, was to be the field color, and a deep, Yankee blue was to outline the trim. Then they had repainted their house and garage, applied the colors to the new shop, and everything matched.

That was all years ago and as I approached the shop, I could see bits of paint peeling like cedar bark, crying out for a new coat. The door had a large window set into the upper panel, but revealed nothing of the inside in the dwindling light. I tried the knob and was surprised to find it unlocked. I pushed the door open and Morphy went inside, nose first.

A bank of switches by the door fed electricity to two rows of fluorescent lights overhead. They sputtered to life when I flipped the switches up. The fluorescents ran the length of the shop and gave it an industrial feel. Halogen and incandescent lamps were scattered around the bench and by permanently placed machines, to provide spot illumination.

Suspended from the ceiling, between the fluorescent lights, were two racks where Walt stored his long wood stock. Most of it was thin stuff, no more than four inches wide, but almost all of it was eight feet or more in length.

Morphy located an olfactory heaven near the center of the room. There was an island where the table saw was rooted. It was caked with blackened, dried blood. No one had cleaned it up following the accident. And how could they? Wiping, scrubbing, soaking, and washing away the blood, the gory reminder of her husband's or his father's death was not something to be done within hours of finding out. No one could really expect either Margie or Brian to perform the task. Since the mess was still there, I assumed that either Yakima didn't have a service recommended by the police, or that Margie had turned it down. I decided to do it myself in the morning before leaving for Seattle.

I pulled Morphy away from the gory scene. He growled and let out a bark. He'd never gotten angry with me before, and I let him go more from surprise than fright.

"Excuse me?"

I spun around and faced a man standing in the doorway to the shop. He was about five feet six inches, and looked like indoors was the place for him to be on windy days. The jeans he wore had been in their prime probably fifteen years earlier, given the fuzzy faded thighs and white threads dangling from the hole in the left knee. The paunch under his red T-shirt said what food he did eat felt comfortable not migrating to other parts of his anatomy.

"Hi," I said. "What can I do for you?"

"I was going to ask you the same question. My name's Ed Carter. I live next door."

"Oh. Hi. I'm Ray Gordon." We shook hands and Ed gave me a hard look. "I'm Walter's chess teacher."

Ed nodded and smiled. "Okay. He told me about you. I guess we never met. Sorry to sound suspicious, but I didn't expect to see the lights on out here."

"Were you and Walt good friends?" I asked.

"Oh, yeah. That's my stool right over there." He pointed, and I followed his pencil-like finger to a chrome barstool with a small tear in the black leather seat. "On Saturday nights, we'd have a beer or two while he took a break from whatever he was working on. In fact, I think I was the last person to see him alive." Ed slid over to a small fridge tucked under the workbench and pulled out a beer. He twisted the cap off, and in the silence of the shop, it made a loud *pssht*. He offered it to me, but I shook my head, and he took a long pull from the bottle. "I came over to see what he was working on, when I saw him come out to the shop. We talked for a few minutes and I left. About half an hour later, I heard Margie scream." He peeked at the blood on the floor and then back at the wall.

"What was he working on?" I asked.

"Nothing. He hadn't started it yet. He was going to make a frame for something." Ed shook his head and used the bottle to point toward the far end of the shop. "If he didn't have a real project to work on, he made frames. Walt always said, 'It's not a waste of time to practice miter joints.'"

Hanging on the wall and stacked on the floor were hundreds of picture frames, ranging from tiny, for wallet-size prints and dollhouses, to common eight-by-ten and poster-size art frames. Some were plain square sticks. Others were intricately detailed, with carved leaves or ivy crawling around the frame.

"It's funny you're here, though," Ed said.

"Why is that?"

"I helped him pack up a chessboard for you just a few days ago."

5

My chessboard wasn't supposed to be done yet. When I'd first agreed to give Walter chess lessons, and he'd insisted on paying me, I had asked for the chessboard instead of money, under the condition that I didn't receive it until my services were complete. In that way, we would have probably enjoyed ourselves for several years, and both forgotten about the chessboard. I really saw our arrangement as a trade agreement, anyway. He received chess lessons, I got stories about the mother I hardly knew, and we both got to play chess.

"So, what *are* you doing here?" Ed Carter asked.

"It's our scheduled night for a lesson. I didn't know Walt had died, and Margie asked me to stay."

"Gave Brian the night off, huh?"

"Yeah. He looked like he needed it."

"Okay. What are you doing out here, though? Out in the shop."

I shrugged. "I'm not sure. Just looking around. Seeing if I can find anything."

Ed nodded. "I know what you mean. I couldn't believe it when I heard what the cause of death was. Still don't, frankly."

"What do you mean?"

"Well, if you ask me, that old hag Helen—" he pointed his chin toward the back of the shop "—had something to do with it. She lives on the other side of Walt and Margie's fence."

"And?"

"Her husband, Bill, I think his name was, died a few years ago. Drowned or something. I don't remember. Anyway, Helen blamed Walt for it and never spoke to him again."

"Why? How was Walt involved?"

"That's the thing," Ed said. "Walt wasn't even there. I don't know. I'm just running my mouth. She's pretty old, and Walt was pretty big. Anyway, I saw the light and just wanted to make sure everything was all right." He dropped the empty beer bottle in a bin under the bench marked *glass* and it crashed against others. Another bin next to it had the word *cans* stenciled on its face. "Nice to have met you, Ray. Goodnight."

"Goodnight," I said.

Ed stuffed his hands in his pockets, leaving me with a James Dean pose before he disappeared out the door. I stared after him, trying to think. In the year or two I'd been visiting Walt and Margie, I couldn't remember either of them mentioning a friend of theirs dying. Their friend Bill must have died some time ago.

I turned my attention back to the table saw. Blood smeared the surface where Walter's body had been found. It striped the gray metal legs and had been sopped up by the sawdust on the floor. Oddly, as I stared at the pool of blood beneath the saw, I saw the silhouette of George Washington used on the quarter, right down to the little ribbon tying his ponytail.

I shook my head and looked around the shop. Just as Brian had said, a thin piece of wood stock was angled down from the rest of the boards in the rack above the table saw. There were several stools and chairs about the workspace, any of which could have been the one Walter had stood upon. Presumably, whichever one it was had been righted and pushed out of the way at some point during the commotion to save Walter's life, or after the police did their walk-through of the scene.

The more I stared at the table saw, though, the more I had a feeling of something being wrong. But I certainly wasn't a woodworker. In high school, I took a study hall period instead of shop class. That wasn't to say I couldn't find my way around a screwdriver. I knew the difference between a slotted head and a Philips head. However, the types of tools Walter stocked his shop with and used on a regular basis were the kind found on PBS home improvement programs. The only reason I knew it was a table saw, was...well...it was a table with a saw in it.

Then I realized what was wrong with what I was staring at. The blade itself, a ten-inch diameter disc with razor sharp serrations running around the outer edge, was poking up through the slot undeterred. Where was the guard? The question, unfortunately, floated away as soon as I asked it.

Somewhere, I'd read the human brain retains ninety-nine percent of the information it comes across. It's just a matter of figuring out how to retrieve a specific bit of data.

By asking myself the same question I'd asked Walter the first time he showed me around his workshop, I regurgitated the answer.

Walter Kelly had been working with wood and the power tools of the trade longer than most people stick to anything. "Blade guards serve a purpose, Ray," he'd said. "They keep amateurs and young home owners who want to make improvements from cutting off their fingers or losing an eye."

"People like me," I'd said.

"Don't get me wrong. I'm all about safety first, but the plastic blade guards don't always let me see what I'm doing, and I don't get an accurate cut. In fact, this piece right here—" he pointed to a thin shank of black metal "—is where the plastic shield attaches. As you push your wood past the blade, the guard rises over the top, and the piece of metal it's attached to separates the wood. It's supposed to keep the saw blade from binding."

I'd nodded, getting the basic picture as Walt had moved his hands above the saw to imitate the process. "Okay. If it makes it easier, where's the one for your table saw?"

Walt had smiled, like a magician knowing which question was about to be asked, and pointed to a short stack of black metal shanks and plastic shields under his workbench. "I've been doing this too long, Ray. I had one of those separators catch on a knot once. The blade bound up and sent the piece I was working on back at me. Hit me like a bull. I thought it went right through my gut. I've learned they're not for me. But if it wasn't for those blade guards—" he'd smiled "—it would take me a little bit longer to spot an amateur when I walk into his shop."

I wondered if Walt had time to regret not using blade guards in the seconds it took him to fall onto the table saw. Or did the life flashing before his eyes end with him laughing at the power switch on the table saw as he dragged a stool over?

My brief affiliation with the Seattle Police Department had left me with a curiosity about accidents and crimes. With accidents, especially those resulting in death, the first question is, "What in the world was the person thinking?" And since my question for criminal acts is the same one, I guess I've always thought of miscreants as accidents waiting to strike.

I left the police force after I'd killed a fleeing suspect. It was an accident, but I'd had to ask myself, what was I thinking? I'd fired at a man's back. I'd aimed low, but he'd tripped at the most inopportune time.

I'd been on the job less than one month.

My superiors had assured me they had no intention of terminating my employment, but it was a mistake I was too afraid of repeating. If I'd given the mayor a parking ticket, I probably could have lived with myself, but I'd killed a man before I'd even wrinkled my uniform.

Would Walt Kelly have been standing above a running table saw if he'd slipped and almost died the first time he did it? Probably not. But it didn't answer my question. What in the world was Walt thinking?

None of it made any sense. Why would Walt leave the saw on? I did a mental shrug and looked around the shop again, thinking maybe a beer did sound good after all. Instead of the mini fridge though, my line of sight settled on an old broom leaning against the doorframe. The yellow paint on the handle was rubbed away where hands had gripped it many times over the years, and the bristles were splayed every which way, like broken fingers jutting out at unnatural angles. Toward the top of the handle, about two inches down, a hole had been drilled through.

If anything, Walt's wood shop was organized. On the wall the shop shared with the garage hung several long-handled tools. There were three shovels: a spade, a flat edged, and a snow shovel with a bent handle; a rake with a fan of bright orange plastic tines; a Weed Eater; something I couldn't even begin to identify with yard work; four yellow electrical extension cords coiled and looped over a long wooden peg; a shop broom; and a red plastic dust pan. Closer inspection of the wall revealed a long nail set at a slight upward angle next to the dustpan. Yet the broom was by the door.

While the shop itself was orderly, it was far from spotless. There was sawdust, not piles of it, but the finer material had drifted against the feet of the workbench. Dust and curly wood shavings were scattered in corners, along with bits of paper and colored plastic I guessed to be remnants of packaging material.

As I glanced around, I had a vision of a room, empty but for one person with a can of paint and a brush. The floor was white, with the artist on hands and knees painting swaths of blue. Looking up from the floor, the person noticed he had imprisoned himself on a ragged island of white jutting from the corner furthest from the door. I remembered seeing it when I was a child watching Saturday morning cartoons. The cartoons were often interspersed with little snippets of educational material like that, so we kids would learn to never paint ourselves into a corner — both physically and ideologically.

I looked at the broom by the door, and then the floor. I walked around the shop with my gaze cast down until I arrived back at the door. There was little or no sawdust on the floor just under the workbenches, the table saw, drill press, and other big tools I didn't know the names of. Someone had swept his — or her — way out the door. A witch and her broom? What Ed Carter had said about Walt was right. He was a big man. The last time I'd seen Walt, about a month earlier, he pushed three hundred pounds. Could an older woman push him down and hold him to a table saw? I put the witch on the other side of the fence on my mental list of people to visit, and closed the shop door behind me.

6

The next morning, Margie was awake at five thirty a.m., brewing coffee and making pancakes. My mother used to make pancakes every Saturday, and after she died, my uncle Dave continued the tradition until I went to college. With that kind of Pavlovian training, whenever I smelled the sweetened batter, I thought it was Saturday morning.

I stared at the red digital display of the alarm clock by my bed and listened to the hum of warm air being pushed through the ducts. When the clock read five forty-five a.m., I forced myself out of bed. Not only had Margie made me believe it was Saturday, she also had me conscious three hours before I liked to be.

"Margie," I said, as I shuffled into the kitchen and slumped into the breakfast nook by the window, "you didn't need to make breakfast."

"Good morning to you too, Raymond," she chirped. "Actually, I make breakfast every morning."

She flipped four pancakes on the griddle, then stacked them on a plate. She set the plate in front of me, filled my cup with coffee, then slid a serving tray crammed with butter, syrup, sugar, cream, and orange juice into the middle of the table. I spotted Morphy in the living room lying at the foot of the chair with one paw draped over his eyes. Even he preferred sleep to food at this hour.

"I had a little chat with your neighbor last night," I said.

Margie sat down across from me and smeared butter over her single flapjack. "You mean Eddy?"

I nodded. "He thought I was up to no good out in the shop. He came over to make sure things were okay."

"You were in the shop?"

"Mm-hmm," was all I could manage with a mouthful of pancake.

"I'm sorry. I haven't had time to…"

"Don't you worry about that, Margie. I'll take care of it."

She regained her composure after a sip of coffee. "Well, it was nice of Eddy to be on the lookout."

"He told me Walt was done with my chessboard. Is that true?"

"Oh, Raymond." Margie smiled. "Walter finished your chessboard a few months after you two started playing chess."

"I thought we'd agreed that I wouldn't get the board until we were through with the lessons."

Margie put down her cup and ran her finger around the rim of her plate. "Well, Walter always needed something to work on. He may have made it early, but he didn't give it to you, now did he? Besides..." She sighed, blinked quickly, and looked out the window into the steely blue dawn. "I don't think there's any point in worrying about something like that now."

"Margie, I'm sorry. I'm still half asleep. I didn't mean to say..."

"It's all right, Raymond. This is something we all will have to get used to."

"These pancakes are excellent."

She smiled. "Thank you."

After breakfast, I showered, then slipped into Walter's den. The sun was just beginning its daily adventure, and the window came to life with the pink-gray light of dawn. I flipped the switch by the door, and two rows of halogen track lights lit the rest of the room with wide circles of warmth. I sat at the chess table and brought out my binder of correspondence games.

Correspondence chess is a nice leisurely way of playing the royal game. It's similar to the difference between being jarred and battered to get a drink in a noisy bar, or relaxing poolside in eighty-seven-degree heat and having a tall, cool, fruity concoction brought to you.

Chess comes in several forms to suit the needs of everyone. Tournaments use clocks and usually allot each player two hours to complete forty moves. Then the rest of the game must be completed in one hour. Blitz games, on the other hand, give the players only ten minutes or less from start to finish.

A game between friends doesn't need to be timed at all and can take place anywhere, while correspondence games are fought out through the mail. But correspondence matches use time regulations, as well. For every ten moves, the players can take up to thirty days.

While my mailman thought it was ridiculous to spend so much time to play a game, it certainly gave me the time to immerse myself in some excellent chess.

It was within the slower games, the contests that allowed prolonged thought and ingenuity, that the game transformed into an art.

I brought out the postcards I'd received in the mail the previous afternoon and found the games in my binder.

The ability to play a game of chess through the mail relies on chess notation: a system of letters and numbers representing the squares on the board, the pieces themselves and the moves they make. To the uneducated eye, chess notation looks like a cryptic code.

For example, after reading his mail, the FBI kept Humphrey Bogart from playing correspondence chess in 1943 because they thought the chess notations on his postcard games with GI's were secret codes he sent into Europe. Bogart was reportedly an expert-level chess player, and it was his idea to make his character in *Casablanca* a wood pusher as well.

People don't even need a board and pieces to play. It's like being able to record a movie with a DVR even if a television set isn't present. It can be very entertaining to watch people try to figure these conundrums out.

Since my brain wasn't exactly perfect, though, (I've never been able to keep more than a few of my correspondence chess positions in my head at once), I played through the game on the board until I reached the last move I'd sent my opponent. On the back of the postcard was his reply move. I noted it in my binder, then made the move on the board.

BLACK

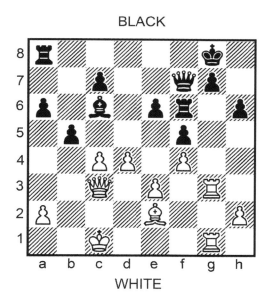

WHITE

My opponent had moved his black pawn to the b5 square, which surprised me, actually. What it allowed me to do was capture his pawn on g7 with my Rook and place his King in check. It was a risk because it forced his Queen to recapture the Rook — otherwise I'd just take his Queen and he would have nothing in return. Once the Black Queen recaptured on g7, I could take it with my other Rook, and then his King would in turn take my second Rook. The risk was that I would be exchanging two powerful pieces for his single most powerful Queen. Would I still be able to hold out?

I stared at the board for another forty-five minutes looking for possible moves, tactical stabs, and possible dangers from the enemy camp. In the end, I wanted his Queen. I took out a blank postcard and addressed it. On the back, I recorded the day I received his move and the day I would send my reply. Then I jotted down my move, 24. *Rxg7 check*, in my binder as well as on the card.

The next few minutes I spent playing through the moves of the game that led up to the most recent. Once the position is set up and ready for my attention, I liked to take a short break to clear my head. At home, I might look over my music collection and put something "chessic" in the stereo, like Beethoven or Wynton Marsalis. At the Kelly household, I only had Walt's den, but I wasn't a woodworker and none of his chess books were new to me.

I decided to call Carla Caplicki. Carla and I had known each other since high school. We'd been lab partners in sophomore biology (and any other subject where the students were forced to work together). Since our relationship was based on actual schoolwork, Carla had been the only girl I could talk to without hyperventilating. My entire adolescent life had been spent either over a chessboard or hanging out with neighborhood buddies. Girls had been in a realm that involved feelings and emotions, things that had stirred up thoughts of my parents, things I'd been too afraid to reveal to myself, let alone a girl. In retrospect, if I'd taken more classes without Carla, maybe I would have met more girls.

Carla and I had both attended the University of Washington as well, but her ambitions leaned toward public service in a different capacity than mine did. She'd eventually landed at the King County Courthouse, and I went to the police academy. Not only was she able to help thousands of people each year with their taxes, assorted licenses, and myriad other types of county business, she also waged her single-woman war against paperclips.

With a job involving masses of paper and bunches of documents moving from person to person and office to office, Carla had developed a festering dislike for the small twists of metal. She complained about tiny rivulets of torn paper, cluttered desk drawers and the disappearance of important papers because some doofus in another department tried (and failed) to clip too many pages together.

Carla used small binder clamps and urged everyone in the King County Courthouse to follow her lead. Not only did she spread her message by word of mouth, she posted colorful flyers on bulletin boards renouncing the use of paper clips, she signed her e-mails with "Paper clips make me flip," and directed people to her web-site, www.paperclipsgetbent.com, which was dedicated to ridding the world of the paper clip scourge.

I looked at my watch and smiled. There was no way she would be awake at this hour. I called Carla's number on my cell phone. It rang six times before she picked up.

"Hello?" she mumbled, drawing it out as if she was trying a new language.

"Hi, Carla," I said with my best game show host voice. "Good morning!"

"Ray? What time is it? It's dark outside."

"Well, you told me to call you when I had a chance."

"So you call now? What are you doing awake at this hour?"

I filled her in on Margie's morning ritual and then told her about Walt.

"Oh, Ray." Her voice was clearer as she woke up. "I'm sorry. This hasn't been a good week for you, has it?"

"Not really."

"When's the funeral?"

"This afternoon. At two."

"You okay?"

"Yeah. This just wasn't something I expected."

"How was Erica's funeral?" she asked.

"It was nice." I wondered how she remembered the names of the kids I dealt with at the youth center. "Jason had some family there, anyway. Hopefully none of them are as bad as his parents. There were some picketers, too. They want Mom and Pop Minor to get tried for murder."

"Yeah, I saw that on the news. Won't happen, though. They're so fried, any decent lawyer will be able to argue incompetence." She yawned into the phone, which made me yawn back. "When will you be back?" she asked. "You still need a tux."

I winced. A week earlier, Carla had begged me to be her date at a wedding she wasn't only attending, but at which she'd also been asked to be the Guest Book Hostess. "It just wouldn't be proper to be *in* the wedding and not have an escort," she'd said.

I'd rolled my eyes and said, "You're not *in* the wedding. You're just asking people you don't know to sign a book. I thought little sisters or cousins did that."

"Ray, she asked *me!* Please?"

"How long have you known about this?" I'd accused, though lightheartedly.

Silence.

"Okay…who's the second choice, you or me?"

"Me," Carla had said glumly. "The Maid of Honor's little sister was going to do it, but now she has a volleyball game."

I'd smiled to myself. At least I wasn't the pinch hitter on Carla's dating line-up. "What color is your dress?"

"Green." She'd made a Mr. Yuck face.

"I'm in."

That was over a week ago, and I was still tuxless.

"I'll be back either tonight or tomorrow. It'll depend on how I feel after the funeral," I told Carla over the phone. "We can go on your lunch break, okay?"

"Okay. And Ray? Please don't call me this early ever again. Or else."

"That's cute." I pictured her acting tough in her pajamas, then felt my face redden.

"You're buying me lunch, bub. Good night."

I hung up, and sat at Walt's desk. The bigger drawers on the sides were stuffed with personal records, accounting items, and household interests. In the thin middle pullout where most people kept pencils and pens, I found a short stack of plastic credit cards. I shuffled through the Visas, Master Cards, and membership IDs until one struck me. It was blue and white and said Yakima Valley Regional Library. Margie said Walt had gone to the library the night before he died. Obviously, she was right in thinking he wasn't telling her the truth. If he had gone to the library, his card would probably have been on top of the stack.

I slipped the library card into my pocket and replaced the rest in the desk drawer. Behind the stack of credit cards was a business-sized envelope stuffed to near bursting. I pulled it out and looked inside. Layers of pink sales slips, all with the same company name—Meyer's Lumber—were lined up like the gills of a fish. I thumbed through them and saw different amounts ranging from fifteen bucks here to five or six hundred there. The common denominator was they were all credited to an account. None were stamped "Paid in full."

I added it up, then pushed the envelope to the back of the drawer. Walt owed over five thousand dollars to Meyer's Lumber.

The next one and a half hours I dedicated to chess and finding the single best move against my next correspondence opponent. He was an older gentleman of seventy-three who lived in the heat of Arizona. His name was Earl Thomas, a retired dentist whose wife was "as hot as a flat rock in the desert." Whatever that meant. When Earl had written that particular bit of information at the bottom of a postcard, I was inclined to ask if flat rocks retained more heat than round ones, but decided I didn't want to get any more geographical metaphors sent my way.

According to the card in my pocket, the Yakima Valley Regional Library opened its doors at nine a.m. At nine fifteen, I left Walt's den and found Margie drinking a cup of tea and watching *The Price is Right*.

"Margie, would you mind if I went out for a bit and left Morphy here?" I asked.

"Of course not, Raymond." She stared straight ahead, her focus locked on the carnival that was the TV show.

"Can I get you anything while I'm out?"

No reply.

"Margie?"

"It's okay, Raymond. Morphy and I will have a nice snack."

"Not too much. He's staying inside while we're at the funeral," I said, and went out the front door.

Ed Carter stood in his driveway, next to a small white Ford Focus I hadn't seen the night before. On the door was an image of a tall pine tree in front of Mt. Rainier. "Washington State Department of Health" was written next to it.

"Hi, Ed," I said. "Or do you go by Eddy?"

He wore black slacks and a white short-sleeved dress shirt divided by a thin black tie. A little hair gel gave him a geeky look, but without a pocket protector, it didn't put him over the top.

He tossed a manila folder onto the passenger's seat of the Focus and closed the door. "Only my close friends and my grandma call me Eddy," he said. "I know you're not my grandma, but since you're keeping an eye on Margie, and apparently she mentioned my name, you must be a friend." He smiled. "Ray, right?" I nodded. "How's Margie doing this morning?" he asked.

"She made pancakes and is watching *The Price is Right*. I guess that's normal."

"Yeah, that sounds about right. Are you going to the funeral?"

I nodded again. "Yes, but I want to go to the local library first. What's the fastest way from here?"

"Go up to Lincoln—" he pointed north "—turn right and follow it all the way down to 2nd Avenue. Turn right on 2nd and you can't miss it."

"Thanks."

"What's at the library?" he asked.

"Chess books." I climbed into the Land Cruiser. "Can't resist 'em."

7

■ The Yakima Valley Regional Library occupied the corner of two one-way streets at 3rd and A. From the outside, it looked like it was built along with the myriad of other public buildings in the late nineteen fifties and into the sixties to look both modern and futuristic: pale, sand-colored bricks formed a perimeter around the base of the library and came up about waist high; a cement wall, painted a shade of sky blue usually reserved for mental wards and elementary schools, was interrupted by rows of squat, metal-paned windows.

Somewhere in the world an old architect who graduated at the bottom of his class laughed his ass off every time he passed a public building like this and remembered how he pulled a fast one on the bureaucrats.

Inside, the library was just as bad. Gray light filtered through yellowing curtains, white globes of glass containing oddly-shaped fluorescent tubes were hung too high, and the bookshelves, metal behemoths screwed and bolted together like an Erector Set, were painted the same ghastly blue as the outside.

I think it's sad when a community lets its library go.

At the front desk, I flashed Walt's library card and asked the attending librarian if she could look up my last checkout.

"Oh, my. I hope we didn't lose a library book." She wore a long brown wool skirt that looked like an army blanket and a thick gray sweater a shade darker than the bun in her hair. Her purple lipstick looked like it had been applied by Van Gogh, and she'd left a thick crescent of it along the rim of her coffee cup.

"We hope we didn't, either," I said. "I lent some books to a friend of mine who lives out of town and I can't remember the title of the one I borrowed from the library." She stared at me with watery eyes. "I remember the cover," I tried.

The librarian rolled her eyes like an exasperated high-school English teacher and swiped the card. She tapped a few keys on her computer and handed me the card back. "There's no activity on your account, Mr. Kelly. Perhaps we already turned in our book, hmm?"

"Perhaps we did," I said. "Thank you."

I walked over to a long table where a row of eight computers stared at the rest of the room. Another group of five were wrapped around a circular table like chunky square teeth on a cog. In between the two tables, at a small, gray metal desk covered with software manuals and rubber-band balls, sat a young guy with explosive hair, wearing a faded red-and-white flannel shirt. He was probably a grad student doing volunteer work as a computer tech or customer service guru. His eyes were droopy. He was no doubt bored from answering simple questions by the technologically challenged.

"Excuse me," I said, standing in front of his desk.

He looked up from a black and yellow book and aimed the title, *Internet for Dummies*, at me. "How can I help you?"

"Are you reading up for yourself—" I pointed at his book "—or trying to come down to us mere mortals?"

He smiled and laid the book down. "No comment."

"Did you happen to be here last Friday night?" I asked.

"All night."

"Do you remember an older gentleman, sixty-five years old, big, about two hundred-eighty pounds, dark gray hair?"

"Did he come in to use the computers?"

"I have no idea. Maybe."

"Lots of older dudes come in by themselves to surf for porn. I guess their old ladies—pun intended—don't let 'em look at home."

I had no idea if Walt would come to the library for Internet porn. I doubted it, but who knows?

The kid shook his head. "They get all mad because those sites are blocked. I can always tell. Their faces get red and they look around like they wanna ask what the deal is, but they're too embarrassed and they leave. It's hilarious, man."

I stared at him. "Big guy. Sixties. Any ideas?"

"Friday night, huh? I remember a couple of old guys coming in. Not real big, though."

"Thanks," I said.

The library was a bust. Margie knew Walt hadn't come to the library, but I had to make sure. He'd gone somewhere Friday night, but where? Often, when people told a lie, there was some truth hidden within it. Walt had lied about going to the library to look something up. The question was: was the hidden truth about finding information, or about where he went that night?

It was close to ten thirty in the morning, and my curiosity had me by the scruff of my neck. It made my next stop the Yakima Police Department, a sprawling brick and glass structure squatting over two city blocks. One thing the police did not like was having their investigations questioned. And why should they? No one liked to have their work sniffed and prodded at by outsiders who thought they knew better. The fact I was once a man in blue didn't matter. It would just sound like I thought I was superior; I decided not to even mention it.

Through the glass front door, I entered a bright atrium with a ceiling that towered above the rest of the building. Two walls were all glass, interrupted here and there with structural beams designed to give the space an industrial feel but remain aesthetically pleasing.

The atrium was divided down the middle by a heavy iron hand rail, which meant people leaving the police station could walk right out while those of us going in had to pass through a metal detector and have our pockets and bags searched. The experience was not unlike airport security, except the police allowed me to keep my shoes on.

The main lobby of the Yakima Police Department was another high-ceilinged room. It had a wide U of teal-colored padded chairs for visitors. Three service windows labeled Municipal Courts, Police Department, and Administration were spread over three walls and divided by racks of pamphlets and anonymous doors.

I went straight to the Administration window and stood in line behind a woman whose body, from the top of her head to the drop of her buttocks, was shaped like a potato. Beneath the potato was a mini-skirt made of wonderfully stretchy fabric and two thin, almost shapely legs wedged into four-inch-tall platform sandals.

When I was a kid, I used to watch a show on Saturday afternoons called *Creature Feature*. It aired old black-and-white horror movies with monsters that were usually created with a variety of parts, or through a scientific accident. I shook the memory out of my head as Frankenstein's Potato walked away, and I stepped up to the window.

A young woman wearing a sweater with a cloth badge sewn on the lapel greeted me happily through a two-inch-thick sheet of glass with a small slot at the base. I didn't know if she was a civilian or a cop, but she certainly didn't look like a vegetable.

I bent slightly toward the open slot and said, "I was wondering if I might be able to talk to someone about the Walter Kelly death last Saturday."

"I'll see if the chief investigator is available. Have a seat over there. It might be a few minutes." She smiled.

I sat in one of the bluish seats and perused a leaflet urging me to not carry illegal weapons like Uzis in the trunk of my car.

A few minutes stretched into fifteen. Just when I was learning how to start a Block Watch program in my neighborhood in another pamphlet, Sgt. Dade appeared and introduced himself.

"Ray Gordon," I said, shaking his hand.

"Sorry I took so long. We're a bit understaffed at the moment." Dade stood about six-four, and had a head of jet-black hair sprinkled with gray cropped close to his skull. He was big, too; not fat big, but pro-wrestler big. His arms worried his uniform's shirtsleeves, and he took care not to crush my hand in his grip.

"No problem. I appreciate your taking the time to see me," I said.

I was given a clipboard to sign and a plastic ID badge that labeled me as a *visitor*, and then Sgt. Dade escorted me into the inner workings of the police department. We stopped by his desk where he picked up a yellow pad of paper, a pen, and a manila folder, then continued to a small conference room.

"Okay, Mr. Gordon," Dade said once we were seated across from each other, "What can I do for you? I understand you want to discuss the Walter Kelly case."

I nodded. "Walt was a friend of mine. I live in Seattle and only see him about once a month or so. I was just wondering if you could fill me in on what happened. Margie isn't really ready to talk about it yet."

"Can't blame her. After what she saw, she probably won't ever talk about it." Dade opened the folder and looked over several pages of reports. "Well, I can tell you Mrs. Kelly called 9-1-1 at twelve thirteen p.m. to report her husband was injured. Emergency vehicles responded, including myself. I arrived on the scene at twelve twenty, just before the paramedics. Mrs. Kelly directed me to the shop, where I found Walter Kelly lying face down on a table saw."

"Sergeant," I said, "I'm not a reporter for a TV station. What can you tell me that's not a run-down of the chronological facts? What happened? What do you think happened to Walt?"

His gaze went from me to the door and back again. "From what we could determine, it looks like Mr. Kelly was the victim of an accident."

"Doesn't it strike you as odd that he would leave a table saw on while he got a piece of wood?"

"Very. But according to his son, Mr. Kelly was known to do that. Besides, there was no evidence of forced entry, a struggle, or any other indication someone was there when it happened."

I started to ask about the broom by the door to the shop, and then thought better of it.

"What is it, Mr. Gordon? Do you know something about the case you're not telling me?"

"Something about this just doesn't feel right to me," I said.

Sgt. Dade sat back in his chair and crossed his arms. "And you want to make sure we covered all the bases."

"Walt was a friend, that's all. Would you mind if I just got a copy of the report? Call me curious, or just wanting to better understand what Margie's going through."

Dade looked at the door again. "As a friend of the family, I'll let you have a look—" he slid the folder across the table "—but it stays here. No copies."

"That's fine," I said. "Thanks."

8

■ The police hadn't found anything to suggest Walter's death was anything more than an accident. Walt and Ed Carter's fingerprints were found in abundance — Eddy's mostly by the mini-fridge — and a few belonging to Margie. Nothing was missing, broken, or otherwise vandalized. No one saw or heard anything unusual. There just wasn't any reason for the police *not* to label Walter Kelly's death an accident.

There was a name in the report that caught my eye, though — Randy Meyer, owner of Meyer's Lumber. A witness had seen a company truck parked across from Walt and Margie's house on the morning of Walt's death. The police had interviewed him and found nothing suspicious.

But I wasn't with the police anymore.

A misplaced broom and a gut feeling weren't much to go on, but it was all I had. What the police had been able to find painted a fine picture of an accident, but a lack of mysterious fingerprints and eyewitnesses didn't rule out foul play. People could lie, gloves could be worn, suspects could hide from view, stools could be overturned, and sticks of wood pulled from their racks.

Margie Kelly was in the kitchen when I got back to her house. She stood against the counter with a hanky in her hand, her reddened eyes staring at the cabinets.

"Margie?" I said. "Are you okay?"

She wiped her nose and pushed away from the counter. "I'm fine, Raymond. Thank you for letting Morphy stay with me. He's such a good dog."

"Margie, obviously something is bothering you. What is it?"

"Oh, it's just stupid." She scraped a chair across the linoleum and sat down at the small breakfast nook. "Brian came by to drop off your suit. That's all."

"Brian upset you? Or did he hurt you?"

"Oh, dear, no! He, well…he brought up the cabin again. I just can't believe with what happened, he's still prattling on about it."

"What cabin? What are you talking about?" Morphy plodded into the kitchen and leaned against my leg, so I could scratch his neck. "Margie?"

She sighed, her shoulders drooped, and she stared out the window. "In nineteen seventy, Walter bought a cabin with two of his friends, Don Harris and Bill Parker. The three of them would go up there all the time for hunting and fishing trips, and every summer, each family could have it for weeks at a time.

"After Bill was killed in an accident, and Don passed on from cancer, Walter never went back. He just didn't feel right about using the cabin without them around. Brian thought he was foolish to hold on to it if he wasn't going to use it."

"Brian wanted Walt to sell it?" I asked.

Margie nodded. "We owned it outright. After Don and Bill were both gone, we bought their shares."

"What happened to Bill?" I remembered what Ed had told me.

Margie sighed. "It was just awful," she said as I sat down across from her. She looked into her teacup as if conjuring memories. "It's not a nice cabin. It's really nothing more than a shack. I thought Walter would have built on to it or renovated it, but they all agreed to leave it as it was. It had something to do with equal ownership or some such nonsense."

I nodded. "So what happened to Bill?"

"The cabin sits on the shore of a little lake, but there isn't a proper pier. It would have been nice to have a little boardwalk and a platform to put our deck chairs on, but there were only a few planks of wood laid out over some boulders. It was absolutely ridiculous.

"Well, Bill Parker went up there by himself on a Thursday in October several years back. Turns out one of those boards on the water broke. He fell and cracked his head on a rock. The horrible thing is that he drowned. If someone had been with him, he probably would still be alive today."

I got up and refilled Margie's cup with tea. The police report I'd seen mentioned Helen Parker as a neighbor they had talked to. They'd asked if she'd seen or heard anything unusual at the Kellys' on the morning

Walt died. She'd said no and that had been the end of it. Helen Parker was Ed Carter's witch.

Since the police had labeled Walter's death as an accident, I doubted they knew about the cabin and the stony relationship between the Kellys and Mrs. Parker. I wondered too about Brian's interest in the cabin, but Morphy stood up and whined before I could talk more to Margie about it. I opened the fridge and gave him half a cold pancake.

"We need to get ready for the funeral, Margie," I said. "Are you going to be okay?"

"I'm fine, Raymond. Brian left the suit in the guest room for you."

9

The weather on the afternoon of Walt's funeral was clear without a cloud in the sky. It seemed remarkably similar to the day Erica Minor was buried, but in central Washington, the sun ruled and kept the autumn chill at bay until November, at least during the day.

Brian Kelly's suit was a bit large for me. I felt like a boy trying on his father's duds for a part in the school play. Luckily, the extra shirt I'd brought along at the last minute was a button-up, and I paid homage to Walt by wearing one of the three ties he'd owned. Even in her grief, Margie gave my outfit a motherly shake of the head and temporarily hemmed the slacks with pins from her sewing kit. Brian took after his dad in the proportion department, so there just wasn't anything to do about the loose jacket.

When my own parents were buried, I had been only eleven years old and had yet to acquire any sort of dress clothes. The day before the funeral, my uncle had taken me to a men's clothing store where I'd blankly tried on miniature suits, ties, and shoes, all while being measured, pushed, pulled, and scrutinized by strange men who smelled like aftershave and cigarettes.

My uncle had paid one hundred dollars for that first outfit of formal wear, and within an hour of my parents' entombment in the earth, I never saw it again.

Walter Kelly's graveside service was held in a cemetery not three blocks from the airport and across the street from two local television stations, and ironically, a health club. While small passenger planes flew overhead and drowned out the pastor's sermon, I looked around at the attendees and for the second time in less than a week felt like an outsider at the closing of someone's life.

The mourners were stoic, heads bent, hands clasped, most wearing black with an occasional dark blue or gray standout. What struck my eyes, though, were five men, roughly the same age as Walt, early to mid-sixties, and dressed in dusty jeans and plaid flannel shirts. They looked like a backwoods clan that had come down from the mountains to pay their respects.

Margie sat erect in a folding metal chair near the casket. She wore a simple black dress and a pillbox hat with a veil. Her son Brian, his wife, Julie, and their young daughter sat next to her. Brian was statuesque in both his posture and silence, while Julie occasionally leaned over to whisper to their fidgety little girl.

Ed Carter stood just outside the perimeter of the crowd, like a security guard at a rock concert. I was surprised to see him staying so far away, since he seemed to have had a close relationship with his neighbor. A beer or two on Saturdays didn't seem like much, but it was the glue of suburban males everywhere. Plus, Ed had his own stool in Walt's shop.

At least Ed was dressed appropriately. Standing about twenty yards behind him was a woman wearing a snow-cone-yellow dress, her head capped with a wide-brimmed white hat. I certainly wasn't an expert on fashion, but I thought I had a pretty good idea what Miss Manners might say about the lone woman's taste in funeral attire. Not that she was dressed worse than the five Paul Bunyan impersonators, but even I knew the Spring Collection from Kmart wasn't something to be worn at a funeral in October.

When Walt was lowered into the ground, several people moved forward to drop flowers on the casket. As I got closer, the five lumberjacks surrounded the grave. Each of them reached into his pocket and withdrew a handful of sand-colored material. They turned their fists over and released five handfuls of sawdust. The shredded wood landed on the coffin in a puff, and then the men ambled off with sunken shoulders. It was like witnessing an ancient woodworker's pagan burial ceremony.

I'd brought along a chess piece, the King from the set Walter and I played with. At the sharp edge of the grave where the grass overlooked fresh earth, I paused and thumbed the points of the cross on top of the piece. Would Walt really appreciate the chess piece, or would he think it was petty of me not to leave the entire set? Or—and I thought it more likely—would he be horrified that I left a beautifully carved King in the ground with him, making an otherwise capable army of chessmen leaderless?

My dilemma seemed to be holding up the line of mourners. Some people went around me or to the other side of the hole, but finally the minister snuck up behind me and draped his arm over my shoulders.

"Everyone must pass and we need to let them go," he said sagely.

I nodded and dropped the King. It landed in the pile of sawdust with a hollow *thump*. The pastor patted my back. "Tomorrow is a new day," he said.

Privately, I said my goodbye to Walt, then moved with the rest of his friends toward the parade of parked cars. The woman in the yellow dress had vanished, and as I climbed into my SUV, I wondered if it was a tradition of some kind to wear bright colors no matter the occasion in the "Palm Springs of Washington." It was one thing to be a happy person, but there were plenty of people in the cemetery who had buried their friend and cheery colors wouldn't hide that fact.

I arrived at Margie's house before she and Brian made it back, and let Morphy into the backyard to pee if he needed to. My hostess expected several guests for a quiet reception, and I wanted Morph to be out of the way. Margie had welcomed his company when we first arrived, but I didn't think any of her guests would be keen on getting their crotch sniffed by a jovial canine. If he got his personal business out of the way, then I could shut him in Walt's den with a bone to keep him busy.

Within a minute of my shutting the door on my dog, the Kellys pulled up to the curb in a chauffeured, glassy black Town Car that the parishioners of Margie's church had insisted on providing. Behind it was a string of cars following like the tail of a kite, winding through the streets until they found somewhere to park.

The house quickly filled with old men and women wearing their Sunday best. Their dressy church clothes had been popular during the Nixon administration, so I no longer felt awkward about my baggy outfit.

Margie had prepared several trays of snacks: meats, cheeses, crackers, veggies and dip, and a plate of sugar cookies straight from the bakery. They lay like fallen dominos on the dinette table in the kitchen, where people would instinctively find them. Brian's wife, Julie, was in the kitchen brewing a pot of coffee, and she had put a kettle of water on the stove for tea. She was tall in a "how's the weather up there?" sort of way, and walked carefully, like a praying mantis, upon thin legs. Her hair was the color of pumpkins, and it shifted back and forth like the cleaning strips at an old car wash as she moved around the kitchen. When she spoke, it was soft, but with a rasp that sounded like she'd been born sucking on a Pall Mall cigarette.

"Hi, Julie," I said, "I'm Ray Gordon." We shook hands and she nodded.

"Brian told me about you," she said matter-of-factly.

"Did you two meet in college?"

"Yes. And no, I didn't play basketball."

"Okay."

I put my hands in my pockets, smiled and looked over the snacks on the table. Finally, I was rescued by the arrival of Julie's daughter, who ran into the kitchen and crashed into her mother's knees.

"Kaylee, you're interrupting," Julie said.

"No, no," I said, "it's okay. I need to go check on my dog."

I maneuvered through the people, who stood like reeds as they listened to Margie talk about Walt. She was telling them a story about something that had happened when they were younger, before they were married. I heard the words "ball of fire" and "clown shoes." I wanted to stay, listen, and be entertained by sepia-toned tales, but the overpowering scents of talcum powder and one-hundred-proof perfume shoved me down the hallway to where Morphy was imprisoned.

When I opened the door to Walt's den, I interrupted what looked like a cross between a shopping spree and an inventory assessment. The five men I'd seen at the funeral wearing jeans and flannel were gathered around the desk and perusing the bookshelves.

"Excuse me," I said, and shut the door behind me. "Just what the hell is going on here?"

They stopped their rifling and looked at me. The ringleader of the group, a dome-headed stick figure with a smoke gray walrus moustache, took off his glasses. "We —" he used his spectacles to point out his pals "— are helping Margie go through Walt's things. Who are you?"

I frowned at a Santa Claus-in-training who had snow-white hair and a beard framing his face. He needed another fifty or sixty pounds in order to make the suit fit. He held enough books to go back to college with. I bounced my glare from him to the books, and raised my eyebrows. "Looks more to me like you're dividing up the loot before somebody else gets to it," I said. The five of them glanced at each other, then Santa slid his books onto the desk and stepped away from them. "Does Margie even know you guys are in here?"

They were like a group of schoolboys caught in the act. All but one. Walrus man sat up in Walt's chair and remained defiant. "I asked who *you* were, young man. One of Walt's lost cousins perhaps?"

I hadn't been referred to as *young man* since my college days. Besides, it didn't matter who I was. The question was why five geriatric hooligans had taken it upon themselves to rummage around Walt's den. "Look. I don't care who you guys are, but this isn't the time to be going through Walt's stuff. I'd like you all to leave before I either call the cops or sic my dog on you." All six of us looked down at Morphy who rattled a bone between his jaws while he rolled on his back in the middle of the floor.

"Son," said Walrus man, "you still haven't told us who you are to be ordering us out of this room."

"*I* was Walt's chess coach!" I said. "Now everybody out!"

10

■ The cars that lined the street disappeared one by one and the neighborhood once again looked like a Northwest autumn on a postcard. No one would guess one of its residents had recently died a grisly death.

The reception at the Kelly household hadn't lasted too long. Most of the guests had wanted to be home by eight thirty, meaning they were gone before six. But any amount of time cooped up in a little room was too long for a dog, and mine needed a walk. As soon as I got the front door open, Morphy bounded down the stairs and onto the front lawn as if he'd been held in solitary confinement for the past twenty-four hours. He dragged me over to the same telephone pole he'd marked the night we first arrived, just as Ed Carter pulled into his driveway next door.

Ed stepped out of his little company car and leaned over the top. "The dog's the boss, huh?"

"Yep. How come you weren't at the reception?"

"I had more work to do at the office." He jabbed his thumb at the car.

"I think Margie missed you." I gave Morphy a tug on the leash and leaned across the hood of my car. "Hey, do you know anything about Walt's cabin?"

Ed frowned in confusion. "Sure. Why?"

"When Brian was here earlier, before the funeral…"

Ed's face relaxed and he shook his head. "Say no more. That's been going on for years."

"Do you know where it is?"

"The cabin? No. I've never been there. I was invited a few times, but…" He shrugged.

I nodded. Ed wasn't an outdoorsman. The pale skin of his bony forearms was testament to that. "Thanks, anyway."

I tugged Morphy back across the front of Margie's house and up Chestnut Avenue, while Ed retreated inside his home. At the corner, we turned left beneath an old oak tree that had bulged the sidewalk above its roots. Then I had Morphy slow his gait. Helen Parker's house was the third on the left, and at the end of a long driveway.

Because of the size of the lot and the way the house perched at an angle, the Parker home looked much grander than I suspected it really was. The black asphalt drive went straight back off the street and contrasted nicely with the thick green lawn. It then curved toward the house and widened to meet the two-car garage. The house was a single-story ranch style, with white aluminum siding and a green roof. There were three tall birch trees in the front yard. Their serrated leaves bright yellow, but few had fallen to the ground. Tall plumes of ornamental grasses guarded the gate into the backyard, and the entire property was lined with a white long-board fence.

Morphy and I walked along the driveway, and I could see Walt's shop parallel with the Parker's garage. As we neared the house, I looped Morphy's leash around a fence post and told him to stay and be good. I looked up and saw a shadow move away from the front window.

The witch was watching.

I gave a friendly wave, then marched up the front steps and rang the doorbell. She may have been watching me, but she took her time answering the doorbell. When she did open the door, though, it was with a rush. I felt the air around me get sucked into the house.

Helen Parker was a woman who'd aged like a piece of fruit left in the sun. Her face was dry and pinched, with long erosion lines that ran from her mouth and across her sunken cheeks, disappearing below the collar of her blood-red blouse. When she spoke, her teeth remained closed and only her lips pulled back to let her voice escape. She looked like the mummified remains of an ancient heiress featured in National Geographic. But unlike an unearthed corpse, Helen Parker was tall, just under six feet, and held herself proudly.

"Can I help you?" she asked. If her words had been real, they would have been cancerous, hateful little beings, annoyed at having been spoken aloud.

I tried to keep a neutral look on my face, somewhere between accusation and door-to-door salesman. "Mrs. Parker, my name's Ray Gordon. I'm a friend of Walt Kelly."

Her lips drew back to reveal her teeth in a skeletal grimace and she squinted. "Mr. Gordon," she said curtly, "unless you're dead too, you *were* a friend of Walter Kelly."

"You must be an English teacher," I said. I wanted it to sound like I was impressed by that fact, but it didn't have any effect on her.

"One doesn't need to be a teacher in order to appreciate and expect proper grammar, young man. Now, what do you want?"

It was the second time that day I'd been called *young man.* "May I come in?" I asked, with as much polite grammar as I could muster. "I doubt if you'd want the neighbors to hear."

She looked down her nose at me and pursed her thin lips.

I shrugged. "Okay." I raised my voice and looked around. "I want you to tell me why you murdered Walter Kelly."

"Oh, this I just must hear." She stepped back inside and left the door open.

Helen Parker's living room was white — white walls, white carpeting, white leather sofa. Family photographs and flowery artwork were encased in white frames with white mats, which made the color inside erupt in a frenzy of hues.

I tiptoed across the carpet and sat on the edge of the sofa. Next to me, a furry, white pillow opened its yellow eyes and turned into a cat. The cat regarded me for a moment, and then leapt from its spot before I could pet it.

"How many cats do you have?" I asked Helen as she sat down in a straight-backed chair across from me.

"Four."

That explained a lot, I thought. Helen Parker was a cat person.

"I have a dog," I told her.

"Yes. I saw."

I smiled. When it comes to people with pets, there are dog people and there are cat people. They live their lives by different philosophies and often take on the characteristics of their animals. Dog people are fun loving and a bit more carefree, while cat people tend to be solitary, untrustworthy, and condescending. Helen Parker fit the stereotype to a T. Of course, being a dog person, I might have looked at her with some bias.

"Well," I said, "how do you know the Kellys?"

"We're neighbors."

"Who moved into the neighborhood first?"

"They'd been here a few years before we moved in," Helen said with as much disinterest as she could boil up.

"How did you meet? Did Margie bring you a pie or something as a housewarming gift?"

She nodded. "As a matter of fact, yes, she did. And Walter gave us a birdhouse he'd built. It was the mirror image of this house."

"Nice."

"Yes. Very neighborly."

"And the cabin?"

A shadow passed over Helen's face. "I hated that stupid cabin." She cleared her throat as if the memory made her sick. "When we all went up to look at it, it was all I could do to keep from laughing. I've seen my grandchildren make better 'cabins' out of cardboard boxes and couch cushions!"

I found it hard to picture Helen Parker watching over little kids, let alone having any of her own. The bitterness must have come after her husband's death. "Let me guess, you were against investing in the cabin?" I asked.

"Investing? How is a big plywood box an investment?" she said, wide-eyed. "I told Bill he was out of his mind, but he wanted to go fishing! Had to go fishing! He wouldn't listen to me. Walter had them both talked into it before any of the wives could see it, anyway."

"Did you ever go up there after you first saw it?"

"Once."

I waited for her to elaborate, but she only stared at me. "What happened to your husband?"

"He died," she said coldly. "Eleven years ago. Up in the mountains, all alone at that stupid cabin."

"Did you hate the cabin this much before your husband died?"

Helen fixed me with a stern squint. "Don't patronize me, young man. My husband's passing is nothing to joke about. I thought Walter's idea of a shared property was fine, but what he found and talked my Bill into was ludicrous. Walt was so good with wood, he could have fixed the cabin up into something to be proud of—a real summer destination we would all look forward to visiting. But he wouldn't do it."

"It was my understanding," I said, "that Walt didn't want to fix it up. That way the cabin would remain equal. If he worked on it, it would have become more his."

Helen squinted again and pursed her lips as best she could. "Just an excuse in my opinion." She waved her hand at the very thought. "They all could have contributed something. But Walter insisted, and Bill died. It's as simple as that."

"And you've always blamed Walt Kelly for your husband's death. Just because, in his mind, he was trying to be fair to Bill and Mr. Harris."

"How is my husband dying fair? Walter was selfish and lazy."

"So for eleven years, you've held a grudge, a hatred, and last Saturday it finally exploded. You saw an opportunity and you killed him."

Helen smiled like a fairy tale's wicked queen. "I didn't kill Walter Kelly, Mr. Gordon," she purred.

"Were you at the funeral today?"

"Yes, I was. Wouldn't have missed it."

"Did you happen to wear a yellow dress?"

She smiled again. "I thought the occasion warranted it. Justice has finally been served. Now if you'll excuse me, I'd like to go to bed."

11

■ It wasn't late when I got back from my visit with Helen Parker, but I didn't want to leave Margie alone on the night of her husband's funeral. Even though Brian had been willing to be there, he had his wife and little girl, and I wasn't really in a hurry to get back to Seattle just to go tuxedo shopping, so I stayed another night.

For breakfast, Margie prepared a fruit salad, a bowl of Cheerios, and a slice of buttered toast for each of us. Walt had obviously made his own breakfasts when he was alive. There was just no way he had achieved the mass of a small car by eating toast and fruit. Walt must have been a bacon, sausage, and hash browns man.

Margie was quiet during the meal, and I wondered if Helen Parker had called to rat me out while Morphy and I slept in. "Is something bothering you, Margie?"

"I'm sorry. I didn't realize I was being rude. Just thinking of Walter."

"You don't need to entertain me. Hey, can I ask you, though, who were those five guys who performed the sawdust ritual at the funeral?"

Margie rolled her eyes and shook her head. "Those bozos were friends with Walter. They'd come around at all hours of the day and night to borrow tools or books or trade pieces of wood. I swear the only good thing to come out of all this is that they won't have any reason to hang around here like a bunch of teenagers wasting their time anymore."

"You know I found them in the den going through Walt's binders and woodworking books," I snitched. After the trouble they gave me, and since Margie didn't like them, I didn't mind tattling.

"I'm not surprised. More than once, I thought they were only here for the tools and not Walter's friendship. Those rats. You mark my words, Raymond, those five yahoos will be here wanting everything out in the shop before the end of the week."

Bozos, *rats*, and *yahoos* were strong words for someone like Margie. A faithful churchgoer, Sunday School teacher, and a member of a classic-literature-only book club, she just didn't cater to true foul language. Just the fact she'd resorted to name-calling at all gave me an idea of how Margie felt about those five clowns. "How well do you know them?"

Margie shrugged. "Well enough, I suppose. They've shown up here, unannounced, more often than our own son, slept on the couch when they've been too drunk to drive. Artie's even stopped in on Christmas Day to talk tools with Walter. Christmas Day, if you can believe it!"

"Artie? Which one is he?"

"He's the little toad with the sack under his chin."

Wow. Artie was a man Margie did not care for. The man she described had been sitting on the corner of the desk thumbing through one of Walt's gray binders that was full of sales receipts and owner's manuals. He wasn't fat, but his outstanding feature was a wattle of skin that connected his chin to his chest and looked big enough to house a joey. It jiggled like meringue at the slightest tic. Artie hadn't said anything when I'd confronted him and the others, but he never took his eyes off of me. "Does Artie have a last name?"

"Francis," Margie told me. "Why?"

"He looked familiar to me," I lied, "but I don't recognize the name. Well, thank you for breakfast. It was excellent."

She smiled and started clearing the table. "So, what are your plans now?"

"Ready for me to get out of your hair?" I smiled.

"Raymond!" she said. "Don't say such things."

I laughed. "Actually, I thought about running to the store for a couple of bottles of water and a bone to keep Morphy busy on the way home. Then I'll pack up and head out. Can I get you anything while I'm there?"

My plan actually included finding someplace to stop and get some real food into my belly and then a quick run by Meyer's Lumber Company, which was why I didn't just invite her to come along.

"No, I'm fine, Raymond. I can't think of anything I would need at the store."

I drove east on Chestnut, took a left, then a right onto Summitview Avenue. There were plenty of shops, but I wasn't looking for knick-knacks, jewelry, or DVDs. What I wanted was something hot to fill my stomach. When I finally saw a place I thought might do, I pulled off the road and went inside.

At the counter, I ordered steak and eggs. I took a seat at a booth with hard yellow Formica seats and watched two flies spinning drunkenly from the cool October weather.

What Margie had told me about Brian made me wonder about him. I didn't think of it at the time, but I wondered if he'd wanted to buy the cabin from his father. The value of lakeside property had probably tripled since it was first purchased in the nineteen seventies. Still, Margie said Brian and Walt didn't see eye to eye on certain things. She didn't say anything about an all-out hatred.

Helen Parker, on the other hand, seemed to have a very unhealthy dislike for Walter Kelly. Eleven years was long enough to let anger ferment into something strong enough to poison the soul. Once the soul had been overtaken, reason fell very quickly. She was bitter and she wasn't a tiny, little, question mark of a woman bent over her walker. Under the right circumstances, Helen could have tripped Walt up and pushed him over, or maybe even witnessed the accident but done nothing to stop it. Anything was possible when strong emotions were involved.

My cell phone rang just as I finished my eggs. "Hello?"

"Hey, bud." It was Carla Caplicki.

"Hi, Carla. What's going on?"

"You want to hear some bullcrapaloni?" she asked.

"Who wouldn't?"

"The wedding has been bumped up to Saturday."

"What? How can they do that?"

"The deputy mayor got hit by a bus two nights ago and a big funeral is planned at the mayor's church for Sunday. Guess which church."

"You're kidding."

"Nope. And since everyone is in town for the rehearsal dinner anyway, the happy couple decided to move the big day up rather than push it back. Which means the rehearsal dinner is now Friday night, which means you need to pick up your tux tomorrow."

"Okay. I should be back by six tonight. Hey, can you do me a favor?"

"Of course! But it'll cost you, and remember, you're already buying me luh-unch," she said in a sing-song.

I could imagine the smile on her face. It was obvious. "There should be a package at my house. Could you pick it up for me?"

"Sure. See you tonight."

I holstered my cell phone, gulped what remained of my coffee, and walked out to my car.

Meyer's Lumber Company was a long building painted the same color green as the outfield walls of major league baseball parks. It was old-fashioned in that the exterior walls wore shingles instead of cement, and it looked like a leftover factory shop from the nineteen thirties. There were two doors: one for customers to enter the store where hardware and other supplies could be found, and a larger door, big enough to allow trucks access to the wood stock that was stacked here and stood on end in bins there. The whole place smelled like sawdust and earth, unlike the big, do-it-yourself warehouse stores tacked onto the ends of strip malls.

I went through the larger door and veered into the shop through an interior entrance. The creamy, vinyl tile floor was chipped, and in places, entire squares were missing, revealing serpentine lines of dried up adhesive. There were several neat aisles stocked with tools, planes, measuring tapes, sandpaper, drill bits, and vises. At the end of each aisle were displays of the latest woodworking gadgets, and near the counter was a large, multi-bin, rotating stand that held several sizes of screws and nails in bulk.

"I'm looking for Randy Meyer," I told the young woman at the counter.

"Is he in trouble?"

"Do you ask all your customers that when they ask for Randy?"

She was young, late teens or early twenties. She didn't have a nametag, but she was probably Randy Meyer's daughter. Somehow, a cashier making minimum wage and caring if the boss was in legal trouble didn't seem to fit.

"No." She smiled, looking down and turning pink. "I just know he was out late and you look like a cop."

"Do I? Really?" I straightened out of my slouch and pulled in my stomach. "How exactly does a cop who's not in uniform look?"

"Like someone not covered in sawdust." She smiled. "Hold on, I'll get him."

She slid off of her stool and pushed through a door behind her. I turned and poked around the open bins of nails and screws.

"I'm Randy Meyer," a voice behind me said. "What can I do for you?"

Randy was on the height-challenged side of five-six or so, and wore his tightly curled orange hair in a business-on-top, party-in-the-back mullet, which must have been *the* style at his senior prom. His arms were solid. The way baseball bats are solid. He wore a faded red-and-gray flannel shirt and wide-legged jeans speckled with sawdust and small bits of wood. A yellow plastic tape measure rode his hip. He looked like an angry lumberjack from a Bugs Bunny cartoon. The only thing missing was a knit cap and a mustache.

I introduced myself and we shook hands. "Could I talk to you a minute about Walter Kelly?"

The girl glanced at us both and returned to her perch on the stool. Randy looked at her, and then motioned for me to follow him to the end of the aisle.

We stopped in front of a display of adhesives. Everything from wood glue to polyurethane bonding agents was right there. If I wanted to stick ceramic to metal, wood to rock, or whatever to something else, I was in the right place.

"What is this?" Randy whispered as he spun around to face me. "I already talked to the cops."

"Did you?"

"Yeah. Who are you?"

"I was a friend of Walter's." I shrugged. "You could say I'm looking into his accident."

"Yeah? I think you should look somewhere else."

"I'm not accusing you, Mr. Meyer. But Walt was a friend of mine and I'm just trying to put together a timeline leading up to his death. One of Walt's neighbors saw your truck parked across the street that morning."

Randy nodded and looked at his feet. "That's right. I never denied it. I was making a delivery."

"Okay. Again, I'm not accusing you here, but from what I heard, you were in your truck for quite some time. Now let me tell you how that looks. You were sitting in your truck, either working up the nerve to commit murder, or cleaning your hands and calming down following the murder."

Randy threw back his shoulders and his eyes went wide. "You son of a bitch," he said in a menacing whisper I was sure the girl at the counter heard. "I've had my share of problems with the law, but I've never killed nobody."

I held up my hands. "I understand. All I'm saying is how things could look once the police find out how much money Walt owed you. I just want to understand what happened."

"Okay—" Randy pointed toward the door " —here's something for you to understand—get out of my store right now or I'm going to have more trouble with the cops, if you know what I mean."

I was beginning to think my interrogation skills needed some improvement. Randy didn't wait for me to leave. He turned and stomped up the aisle and stiff-armed the door to the lumberyard.

The girl behind the counter was wide-eyed but otherwise silent. I shrugged like it was no big deal to be threatened and kicked out of a store, and then I went outside.

The street where I'd parked in front of Meyer's Lumber was wider than most. It was in an industrial area, and built to accommodate tractor-trailers, delivery trucks, and service vehicles. Not only was the street extra-wide, but the parking slots for customers were a good car-length-and-a-half away from the thoroughfare. It reminded me a lot of an airport runway, with the buildings set way back from the traffic.

Which was why I was surprised when, just as I turned the ignition over, my car was hit in the rear and spun ninety degrees by a passing forklift.

12

The bozo who'd driven his forklift into the back of my SUV sat in the seat and shook his head like he couldn't believe what just happened. But I knew what had happened, and I wasn't about to let Randy Meyer get away with it. I called the police on my cell phone and reported the accident, then sat in the Land Cruiser and waited for them to arrive.

Randy Meyer ran out of the lumber house and verbally berated his employee with the gusto of a college basketball coach. He even grabbed the front of the driver's shirt and really got into his face. I thought his performance was a bit over the top, but I'm sure Randy felt like he needed to make it look genuine.

Twice, he came over to my rolled up window to plead apologetically, but I ignored him and played video games on my cell phone. The second time, Randy made the mistake of smiling before he turned and walked back to the forklift.

I'd pissed off the wrong guy.

When the police arrived, I got out and inspected the damage inflicted on my Land Cruiser. The rear passenger-side fender was crushed and pushed behind the tire. What remained of the tail light glittered on the asphalt like a shattered cherry lollipop.

I shook my head and looked at the police officer. Rogers was his name. He was older, probably in his late forties or early fifties, and had a belly on him that suggested he didn't run down too many criminals—at least not on foot. He asked me to describe what happened. As I told my side of the story, the forklift driver, Lee was his name, nodded and verified everything.

"Look," Randy said, stepping into the conversation, "this was an accident. I'll pay for the repairs myself. That way we don't need to hassle with insurance. And since you're from out of town, Mr. Gordon, I'll have a friend of mine take care of it for you. He owns a body shop and I'm sure he can have it done for you tomorrow."

The cop looked at me with his eyebrows raised, silently asking if I'd agree to it.

I nodded. "Okay, but—"

Rogers held up his hand to stop me. "I'm going to take Mr. Gordon to a hotel," he told Randy, "then I'm coming back here to make sure everything's kosher."

"Absolutely, officer." Randy smiled.

I took my cell phone out and snapped four pictures, one of each side of the Land Cruiser. Randy told Lee to move the forklift back inside the lumber house, and officer Rogers chaperoned me into the passenger's seat of his squad car. Once we pulled away from Meyer's Lumber Company, I told him where I was staying and gave him directions.

"You know that was probably the right thing to do back there," Rogers said.

"What do you mean? Taking the pictures?"

"Well, that was good, but I meant letting Randy take care of the damage."

"You sound like you know him."

"Know *of* him, actually. Randy Meyer has quite a reputation among the cops in this town."

"How so?"

"He's a mean drunk," Rogers said matter-of-factly. "He has a lot of anger over missed opportunities and takes it out on people dumb enough to challenge him."

"Opportunities? Like what?"

Rogers made a right turn. "In high school, Randy was a wrestler. State champion, actually. Had a shot at college, maybe even the Olympics. Instead, he stayed here and took over the family business. Almost every night he hits the bars, and after having a few, starts challenging guys to wrestle on the dance floor. Of course, when you get two drunk guys wrestling and trying to prove their machismo, it's going to get ugly."

"Why doesn't he just sell the lumber yard if he hates it so much?"

Rogers brought the car to a stop in front of Margie's house and slid the shifter into Park. "Why don't people wear hats anymore, like they did in the thirties and forties? Hell if I know."

I nodded, got out of the car, and walked around to the driver's side.

"My guess about Randy, though," Rogers said out his window, "is it's just too late. He wouldn't know what to do with himself if he wasn't selling lumber like his daddy used to and generally being an ass to society."

I gave Officer Rogers my cell phone number and shook his hand. "Where would we be without mean drunks to be asses to the rest of us?" I said.

He smiled. "I'll give you a call when your rig is done."

"Thanks."

I waved as he drove slowly down the street. When I turned to go into the house, Margie was on the porch, her eyes wide.

"Raymond," she said when I got to the bottom step, "why on earth did the police bring you home? Where's your car? Did something happen?"

Morphy appeared from behind Margie's dress and bounded down the stairs to meet me. "It's okay." I knelt down to rub Morphy's neck. "There was a little accident. My car got hit, and it's in the shop."

"Oh, no! Are you all right?"

"Yeah, but it won't be ready until tomorrow. Do you mind if I stay one more night?"

"Oh, of course you can stay, Raymond."

I still had most of the day to kill, and already I'd had it out with a socially ignorant grunt with a temper and been given a ride home by the police. Neither Helen Parker nor Randy Meyer had given me any reason to believe he or she had murdered Walt, but I certainly couldn't rule one or the other out, either. Both hated him, both were temperamental, and both had opportunity. Then there was Brian Kelly and Artie Francis.

"How about a cup of tea?" Margie asked as I sat wearily on the sofa. Morphy leaned against my legs and I scratched his head.

"I don't recall you ever telling me of your British heritage," I said.

"Well, I think you're just fine," Margie said with a smirk.

I laughed. "Tea would be great. Thank you. I'm going to call Carla while the water heats up."

"Girlfriend?" Margie's eyes brightened.

I frowned, unsure how to answer Margie. How *did* I feel about Carla? "We're not a couple," I said.

There were times when I thought of Carla as more than a friend. We had the kind of relationship where one was always there for the other, like musical notes in a just-so composition. In high school, I'd refused to develop feelings for her or anyone else. I eventually came to believe it was because of the loss of my parents. When they died, I just didn't want to deal with that emptiness, the disembodiment of not belonging to anyone, again.

Margie smiled. "But…?"

"I'm not sure."

Margie grinned like a teasing aunt and turned to go into the kitchen. I shook my head at her, thinking she was a gossip, but she did get me pondering. Carla and I had never gone out on an official date. I'd filled in before, like she'd asked me to do with the upcoming wedding, and she'd done the same for me, but neither of us had asked the other out. We'd never been intimate, never kissed, hugged, or held hands. What were we exactly? Pals?

Friends or chums? Acquaintances? None of those fit. Carla and I had known each other since high school, hung out all the time, yet we'd never made a move to take our relationship to the next level. But Carla was more than my friend, of that I was certain.

Even though Carla worked in the Treasurer's Office at the King County Courthouse, she enjoyed helping other divisions when she could. She could often be found roaming the corridors aiding citizens in need of guidance. So, when I called her now, I was surprised to hear her voice that quickly after I asked for her.

I told her about the accident with Randy Meyer's forklift and how it wasn't really an accident. Margie was a gracious host, allowing Morphy and me to stay another night, but tux rental for the wedding would have to wait.

"You're cutting it pretty close, bub," Carla said. "I'm going to call the tux place and make sure they at least have your size available."

"Okay."

"What are you, forty-two? Forty-four? What?"

"Forty-four, I think."

"Tall?"

"Hey, I'm just a regular guy."

"You are *so* not regular," she said.

She didn't say it with any sort of malice laced in her voice, and after my recent musings about her, I took it as a compliment. I told her I'd call again before I left for Seattle the next day, and we hung up just as Margie's tea kettle whistled.

13

■ Over several cups of tea infused with honey and whiskey — to help me relax after the accident, Margie said — Margie and I talked more about Carla and the incident with the forklift. Then I was able to steer the conversation back to her son Brian, and Walt's cabin.

"What is it about the cabin that Brian doesn't like?"

Margie chuckled. "It isn't just Brian. Nobody liked the cabin, except the three men."

"You're saying Brian wanted Walt to get rid of it? To sell it?"

Margie nodded. "We owned it, but we weren't using it. At all. Brian just didn't understand that and thought it was a waste."

"Why did Walt want to keep it if no one was using it?"

"Sentimentality. That's all. He knew it was silly, but he just didn't want to let it go."

The doorbell rang and Margie excused herself to go and welcome her visitor. My guess was she would have many people stopping by over the days ahead. After I went back to Seattle, she wouldn't be lonely. Already there had been promises from her friends that they would come over to check on her or take her shopping at the mall. All of these arrangements had been made by her lady friends and neighbors who'd attended the reception.

Which is why I was surprised to see Margie lead Artie Francis into the living room. He was dressed casually in khakis and a pink button-up shirt left open at the collar—markedly better than he and his pals were dressed at Walt's funeral—and he dutifully followed Margie with his hands clasped tightly in front of him.

"Raymond," Margie said cordially, "this is Artie. Artie, Ray Gordon."

I stood up to shake his clammy hand and watched his wattle wobble.

"Yes, yes," he said, "the chess teacher."

What was left of Artie's hair was horseshoed around the back of his head. It was a blacker black than anyone his age was entitled to have. He obviously dyed it, which was a mistake, because it made the dandruff clinging to it stand out like grated parmesan cheese.

"Do you live nearby?" I asked Artie as we all sat down.

"I'm out in Selah," he said from his perch on the edge of the sofa.

I nodded. Selah was a small community a short jog to the north of Yakima. I'd never been through Selah because the freeway went around it, but I knew it was home to Tree Top, the apple juice company. It was not a long drive—it only took about two minutes, depending on traffic, to bridge the city limit signs—but Artie had obviously made a special trip.

He wrung his hands and looked from me to Margie and back again. Apparently, he didn't want to broach the subject of tool acquisition with me in the room.

Since nobody said anything to push the conversation along, and I knew Margie wouldn't do anything with Walt's tools until she was good and ready, I stood up and told them I needed a nap. My head throbbed, though I wasn't sure if it was from the accident with the forklift or Margie's spiked tea.

"I'll wake you in time for dinner," Margie said.

"Okay. You know where I'll be if you need me before then." I gave Artie a curt nod and slapped my thigh. "Come on, Morph."

After a dinner of fried ham, baked potatoes, and steamed carrots, Margie and I watched *Jeopardy!* before she said goodnight and went to bed. She hadn't mentioned anything about her visit with Artie Francis other than that he didn't stay too long, so I was confident she was okay with whatever had been said.

I had forgotten to clean up the remains of Walt's accident like I'd intended, so I took Morphy out to the shop to find some cleaning supplies. What I found was something much more interesting than disinfectants and bleaching solutions. At the far end of Walt's bench, in plain view, was one of his books on chess. Why would a chess book be out in the shop? I looked around, but there wasn't a board or a set of chess pieces. I guessed he hadn't been out in the shop studying games or playing against any of his cronies.

I opened the volume to the bookmarked spot and was confronted with the chapter title *The Evergreen Game*. Walt's book contained a move-by-move analysis as well, and I found myself thinking that I hadn't needed to bring my book because Walt had his own.

I shook my head like an Etch-A-Sketch in an effort to erase my thoughts, and focused on the book in my hands. The bookmark Walt had used was a business card that belonged to their neighbor Ed Carter, but on the card, his full name was spelled out—Edward—and in thin, green lettering, next to the same logo that was on his car, his department was listed as Resource Management.

A series of one-by-fours had been mounted like a rail about three feet above the bench and ran the length of the room. It was riddled with thumbtacks, which secured scores of business cards just like Ed's. As I looked closer at the cards, I had to smile. Walt's obsessive-compulsive organization had spilled even onto a seemingly mishmashed business card collection. They were alphabetized, and lo and behold, I was in front of the C section. Walt had probably sat right in the same spot when he'd called and left me the message.

I closed the book and began the gruesome job of scrubbing up Walter Kelly's blood. I doused the dried blood with a liberal amount of lemon-scented ammonia, and scoured the concrete floor with a wire brush. Soon, I'd built up a layer of pink-tinged foam. I gagged from the stench and tried to breathe through my mouth. Morphy had the good sense to lie by the door where some fresh air snuck in under the jamb.

To take my mind off the task at hand, I thought about Brian Kelly. Was it just the cabin going to waste that rubbed him the wrong way, or was it the land value he was afraid of missing out on? Real estate assessments had been big news over the last month or two. Housing prices and land deals had gone berserk, and sellers were making massive profits. Maybe Brian was in trouble financially and he just couldn't take it anymore? Walt refused to sell and Brian killed him for it, knowing the cabin would eventually come into his hands, or he would at least be able to talk his mother into putting the land up for sale.

Outside, I heard Ed Carter's back door creak open and closed. I poured fresh water over the floor and started mopping it up. If Ed planned on being neighborly again, I didn't think he needed to witness the clean-up process. But after several minutes passed without an appearance from the Kellys' neighbor, I began my attack on the table saw with a scouring pad.

Just as I got into a nice scrubbing rhythm, Morphy growled low in his throat and raised his head off of his paws. I stopped and watched him. His ears were erect and his gaze was on the window behind me. Goose flesh erupted on my arms. To hide the shiver that ran down my spine, I resumed wiping down the table saw with calm casualness. I kept my attention focused on Morphy, though, and he growled again. This time, the hair on his shoulders stiffened and rose up as his emotions kicked in. Someone was watching, or trying to look in the window.

Morphy wouldn't get so angry over something like a skunk or a cat.

I twisted around just as Morphy leapt to his feet and barked. Someone ducked down before I could see a face. I ran to the door and pulled it open. Morphy tore around the corner, barking after the intruder, and I followed as close as I could.

In the darkness of Margie Kelly's backyard, I saw Morphy's blond fur disappear into the black shadow of Walt's shop. He chased a dim figure running toward the back of the property to Helen Parker's house. I ran full out once I saw the shadowy form of the person who had been spying through the window. Gone were the trepidations of twisted ankles and bloodied shins from unseen objects lying hidden on the grass.

I ran.

Ahead of me, Morphy made a sharp right turn and vanished into the night. I saw the object of our pursuit vault the fence that followed Helen Parker's driveway and then run across her lawn toward the street. Maybe Morphy had caught a subtle change in the person's direction and planned to cut him off.

Then, in what I would later think of as a profound lesson in physics, my part of the chase ended. I ran into a chicken wire fence, which stopped my legs while my upper body kept traveling forward. Momentum bent me over, pulled my feet up after me and flipped me over. I landed with a *thud* and an involuntary expulsion of breath in Margie's garden.

As I lay there, flat on my back and struggling to refill my lungs, I heard the rumble of a big, throaty engine starting, and the squeal of rubber as my quarry escaped.

Finally, I coughed and breathed in the sweet, cold October air. I raised my knees to my chest and held up my arms. Satisfied nothing was broken, I stayed put, lying on the hard earth, breathing.

After a few minutes of quiet, Morphy trailed up the other side of the chicken wire and sat down behind me. He woofed softly, probably wondering why I had dropped out of the chase, and panted while he waited for me to get up.

14

■ I spent the rest of the evening finishing the cleanup in the shop, and woke the next morning stiff and sore, still wondering who the uninvited visitor could have been. Artie Francis was out because he couldn't have run that fast. The door I heard open and close sounded like it had come from Ed Carter's house. If it had, maybe he went for a walk or was just returning from one. The door could just as easily have been in the Kelly house—Brian Kelly checking in on his mom to find her asleep, and then seeing the light on out in the shop. If he had killed his father, he would certainly have a vested interest in what went on out there. The only thing I couldn't explain was why he would park so far away. As far as he knew, I was gone.

On the other hand, Randy Meyer could have been out snooping around. Officer Rogers did say Randy was quite daring once he had enough booze in him to fuel the fires of stupidity.

And I wasn't really willing to entertain the idea of Helen Parker outrunning me, plus making the leap over her fence. More important than the physical evidence against her, though, Helen struck me as the type of person who would have stood her ground outside the window, as if I was the one trespassing.

At ten a.m., Officer Rogers called to let me know my Land Cruiser was ready. "That was pretty quick," I said. "Does quality count?"

"Sounds like it was an overnight job. From what I could get out of Randy, he told the body shop guy he'd pay extra to do it as a personal favor. Apparently, Mr. Meyer doesn't like you and wants you to go home."

"Well, that's not very friendly," I said.

We arranged for another officer to follow Rogers up to the Kelly house since Morphy wasn't allowed in the patrol car, and then we hung up.

I packed my duffel bag and put it next to the front door. Rogers said they would arrive with my rig in about a half hour, so I decided to push Margie just a little bit more.

"What are you going to do with the cabin now?" I asked her.

"Sell it, I suppose," she said. "I have no attachment to it like Walt did."

I nodded. "What about Brian? Do you think he'll want it?"

"Oh, I doubt it. Not anymore."

"Anymore? Did he want to buy it before?"

"He offered, but Walt knew he'd just sell it."

I bet. The land value alone had probably quadrupled since the nineteen seventies. "Margie, do you think Brian wanted it bad enough to…hurt Walt?"

Margie froze. "How could you suggest such a thing?" She gasped. "You don't know Brian or this family well enough to say something like that. How dare you!" She got up from the table, started to tidy the kitchen by rearranging towels and pushing the toaster against the wall.

"Margie, I'm sorry. I—"

"I think I'd like you to leave now. Thank you for staying these last few nights, but now it's time for you to go."

Sometimes I wonder if I'd had parents into my teenage years, I would have learned when to keep my mouth shut.

15

When they delivered my Land Cruiser to the Kelly house, Officers Rogers and Cruz found Morphy and me sitting on the front curb like a boy and his dog, bored with summer vacation.

"Really anxious, or overstay your welcome?" Rogers smiled.

"A little of both." I pushed myself up and inspected my car, while Officer Cruz kept Morphy company. The fender was smoothed out and shiny and the paint was a perfect match. "Looks like a good job. Hard to believe they did it overnight."

"The tail light assembly was available at the local dealership," Rogers said, "and pulling a dent out is nothing to a guy who knows what he's doing."

"A dent? Didn't you see it yesterday? It was more than a dent."

Rogers shrugged. "Magic elves then."

As the two cops drove away, I threw my duffel bag on the backseat and loaded Morphy into the back. I wondered when the police would receive a report for a vandalized Land Cruiser with a missing rear fender.

I wasn't ready to give up on Brian Kelly yet. There was just something strange about his infatuation with his father's cabin. I drove down to the veterinary clinic where I knew Brian worked, but he wasn't there.

"Dr. Kelly comes in at noon on Tuesdays and Thursdays," the receptionist said.

"A little cold for golf, isn't it?" I smiled.

"I don't think veterinarians play golf."

Walt had shown me his son's house once when we went out to get munchies for our evening chess lesson. I hoped I could remember where it was.

Just shy of eleven a.m., I pulled up to a single-story brick house with a yellow garage door and a cement gnome in the flowerbed beneath the front window. I remembered the yellow garage door.

Before I could knock on the front door, it was opened from inside. A pretty brunette, who might have recently received a college degree (or not), wearing nice-fitting jeans, spilled outside with a giggle and bumped into me.

"Oh! Excuse me," she said.

"The pleasure's all mine." I smiled. "Believe me."

She laughed and tossed a wave over her shoulder as she sashayed to her little red Mazda on the street.

Brian Kelly stood in the doorway of the house. His smile melted when he recognized me, and he crossed his arms. "What are you doing here, Ray?"

"Can I come in?" I asked. "You and I have a couple things to talk about."

His gaze floated up to follow the young woman who just left.

"Don't worry," I said. "It's not about your extra-curricular activities."

Brian didn't say anything. He just turned and walked inside. He did leave the door open, though, and I took that as an invitation.

"What could we possibly have to talk about?" he asked as I shut the door.

I sat down and waited for him to do the same. The living room was oppressive with a six-foot-tall rear-projection television set that loomed out from one wall. A dark brown leather sofa and matching recliner faced the TV, so all who sat might be awed. Covering the back of the sofa was an afghan of crimson and gray—the colors of Washington State University, Brian's alma mater. I assumed it was another of Margie's creations.

A dim hallway led to the opposite end of the house. From where I sat, I could just see the light blue kitchen wall, a small desk with a computer on it, and half of the refrigerator.

Brian finally sunk into his recliner and I said, "Well, I have a dog and you're a vet. There's that, but it's not the reason I'm here." Brian glared at me like a mob boss losing his patience. "I know I'm a smart ass. I'm sorry. Two things. First, all those old guys who were friends with your dad are coming around and looking to get their hands on all the tools. Artie Francis was the first to pounce."

Brian snorted.

"What?"

"Artie Francis doesn't want Dad's tools. He's never built a thing, except maybe a birdhouse when he was in school."

"Then what's he doing?"

"He's after Mom. For as long as I've known him, I would catch him sneaking peaks at her. Jeez, I can't believe he moved this quick." Brian shook his head. "He's probably harmless, but thanks for letting me know."

The "toad," as Margie had called him, had a crush on her. He hadn't come over to discuss buying hardware after all. No wonder she hadn't mentioned their talk.

"What's the second thing?"

"What?"

"What's the other thing you want to talk about?" Brian said. "I need to get to the clinic."

"I want to know what the deal is with the cabin."

"The cabin? *Dad's* cabin? Why?"

"I just left your mom and she's pretty upset." I left out the part where I'd openly wondered if Brian had killed his father. "She said this cabin has been an issue with you for quite some time."

"Yeah? And? Who are you, now? Joe Therapist? This is none of your business!"

"I don't think your father had an accident."

"What? Why not?"

"Something I found in your father's shop. Also, after hearing about this cabin, I'm guessing the land is worth a fortune, and I'm sure you're aware of it, too."

"Are you accusing me of something?"

"No. I'm saying you upset your mother by asking about selling the cabin so soon after Walt's death. Why? Do you need the money to keep your girlfriend happy?"

"Hey! Just who do you think you are, anyway? You're just a guy from Seattle who my dad saw about as much as his barber. You don't know anything about me, him, or my mother!"

"You're right." I stood up, walked to the door, and opened it. "I can tell you need to get to work, anyway."

I didn't want to get kicked out of another Kelly house, and there was no sense in trying to reason with a man who may have murdered his own father—and just got caught with his pants down, so to speak.

From down the block, I watched Brian back his car out of his driveway and leave a small patch of rubber on the street. He drove a big, gray SUV, probably necessary for making house calls to the surrounding farms. I watched the empty street for a few minutes, and then walked back up past his house.

I walked into the neighbors' yard and down the side, where a green wall of arborvitae divided the properties. A quick glance behind me ensured no one was in the street watching, and then I slipped between the bushes.

Brian Kelly's backyard was a neat freak's nightmare: A small fishing boat was mired upside-down next to another row of arborvitae that marked the rear property line; a barbeque flaked black paint onto a concrete patio; and an obstacle course of brightly-colored plastic toys littered the struggling lawn. On the other side of the patio was a rusty tin shed with a padlock on the doors. A metal awning protruded from the house and over the concrete slab, protecting a set of sliding glass doors from direct sunlight.

I intended to commit a crime I had no business committing. Even if I did find something suspicious or incriminating in Brian's house, there was no way I could report it. I had no authority, no right, and no credentials of any kind. I tried the door anyway, and with some effort it slid open. It amazed me how people didn't lock their doors. True, the sliders were a bit rough and could use some oiling, but it was hardly enough to stop a rat in search of some loose cash.

I slipped inside and let my eyes adjust to the sudden change in light. The computer was my first target. I pushed the power switch, and as it hummed and beeped to life, I rifled through the drawers of the desk. There was nothing to pique my interest, just phone bills, car payments, house payments, and other such record keeping.

The computer was a bit more difficult to search than the desk drawers, but I could find nothing about real estate in any of the available documents or spreadsheets.

It was an odd sensation going through a stranger's personal life. I looked at letters to and from relatives and friends, a long list of book titles and authors—whether to read or have read, I couldn't tell—recipes and taxes, pictures, and even some medical essays, some veterinary and some pharmaceutical in nature. I got a quick sense of who these people were without even knowing them. It was like TV personalities.

I double-clicked the Internet icon and was rewarded within seconds. The homepage was a common national news and information site complete with a search function. Another click of the mouse button brought up a history of websites visited over the past week. What I expected was a list of real estate offices and land value sites. What I found was much different. Most recently visited (probably by Brian and his girlfriend) was a porn site called XXX Boots, followed by several funeral related sites and one dealing with the death of a parent. What caught my eye, though, was the long list of sites dedicated to the making and use of methamphetamine.

According to police departments across the country, methamphetamine is one of the worst drug epidemics they've ever faced. It is super-addictive, destroys brain cells the way hot water melts an ice cube, and makes the user do stupid, irrational things in order to obtain more. Methamphetamine is easy to make, but the chemicals involved turn the areas where the drug is made into toxic-waste dumps. When a lab is found, everyone within two blocks is evacuated and a HAZMAT team has to come in and clean the area.

So why was Brian Kelly online learning how to make meth?

16

When I was playing chess with Jason Minor in the hospital, he told me things about his life he'd never shared with anyone. He talked about sleeping with his bedroom window thrown open in the middle of January because the chemical fumes in his house had burned his eyes and nose. He whispered about his parents stealing the twenty dollars he'd received from Grandma at Christmas, and the throngs of strange people who had appeared at all hours. Sometimes, when he'd gone to bed, there would be someone he'd never seen before already under his covers. When that happened, he'd either shared his sister's tiny bed or curled up with a blanket on his beanbag chair.

Jason's parents not only made methamphetamine, they used it and were addicted to it. But not everybody who made meth used it. Maybe Brian Kelly didn't want to sell his father's cabin. If he operated an illegal meth lab, a remote cabin in the woods would be an ideal site. His wife, Julie, was probably involved as well.

The essential ingredient in methamphetamine is ephedrine, a controlled substance used for asthma medications, and sometimes as a dietary drug. Since the FDA controls ephedrine, meth manufacturers use pseudoephedrine, which is found in over-the-counter cold medications. They cook away the "pseudo" using noxious chemicals like ammonia and then combine the result with other chemicals and drugs to arrive at meth. Who better than Julie, a pharmacist, to obtain bulk quantities of meds without suspicion?

I turned off the Kellys' computer and left the same way I'd come in. Once I was back in my car with Morphy, I called Carla.

"Can't get enough of me, huh?" she joked.

"Nothing better than a great assistant."

"Oh, that's low."

"Hey, I'm just about to leave Yakima, and I need to find out where a cabin is. There's nothing but desert over here, so it must be up in the Cascades. Can you do some checking for me?"

"Wow, you're going to owe me big, fella," she said. "These favors are starting to add up. All I need is a name."

"It was originally purchased by three guys in the nineteen seventies. The owner now should just be Walter Kelly, or maybe along with his wife, Margaret."

"I'll call you back."

Instead of driving north to Ellensburg and then west over Snoqualmie Pass, I decided to take Highway 12 toward Mt. Rainier. The quickest way into the mountains from Yakima is over White Pass or Chinook Pass, both of which serve up rivers, pristine lakes, and dense evergreen forests.

Since Walt and his buddies bought a cabin for weekend getaways up in the mountains, I guessed it would have to be along the road west of Yakima.

By the time Morphy and I reached Naches, the last small town before heading into the mountains, Carla still hadn't called back.

On the other side of Naches, Highway 12 branches off to either White or Chinook Pass. Turning south would take me along Rimrock Lake and over White Pass. To the north is Chinook Pass, which leads into Mt. Rainier National Park. Both highways then converge again at the southern entrance of the park.

There was a lot of forest to drive through if I guessed wrong, so I pulled into Naches, bought two tacos for me and a burrito for Morphy, and waited for Carla to call.

We didn't have to wait long. Halfway through my second taco, my cell phone rang. "Hi, Carla," I managed around a mouthful.

"You're eating."

"Mmm hmm."

"Don't ruin your appetite. You're taking me to dinner tonight."

"Does that mean you have some good news for me?"

"A cabin owned by Walter Kelly is located somewhere past Rimrock Lake, but before White Pass."

"That's vague," I said.

"Oh, I can tell you exactly how to get there. How much detail I give you depends on where we're going to dinner."

Detailed directions were relayed after I promised we would dine at the Metro Grill, and I wrote them on a paper napkin.

"Don't be late," Carla said.

"I won't be. It's on the way home."

"Ray, what's this all about?"

"I'm not positive yet, but it might be about murder, drugs, and another little girl in danger."

17

■ Rimrock Lake is a reservoir created after the construction of Tieton Dam. The lake has a clear glassy surface that boaters and water-skiers love, while the controlled river from Rimrock supplies Yakima and numerous communities along its path with water year 'round. Surrounding the lake are the steep peaks of the Cascade Mountain range, covered with pine, cedar, Douglas fir, and other species of trees. It's a haven for wildlife, and I found it difficult not to get caught up in the beauty as I drove along Highway 12.

I turned off the ribbon of asphalt according to Carla's directions and followed a gravel road into the forest. There were several small campsites along the way, and as the road twisted and turned, I felt like the line in an erratic game of connect-the-dots. Morphy lay down to let his burrito settle, and I slowed down a bit more.

After two miles, I came to a spur off of the campground road. This was no more than a path, two ruts separated by a serpentine row of weeds and grass, but it was obviously there, and I did have a 4x4.

I drove slowly, sitting straight to better navigate the primitive road that jostled and bounced us like a carnival ride. Morphy whimpered and grumbled his distaste more than once. I just hoped he'd let me know somehow if he decided to get sick.

After thirty minutes, the light had dimmed significantly and I logically concluded it was due to the height and density of the trees we were among. It wasn't yet three o'clock, but the sun was only just able to touch the tops of the very tallest evergreens.

It was the tops of those trees and the thick butterscotch light I was looking at when I drove off the road. The trees shot skyward as the front end of the Land Cruiser nose-dived into a bramble of salmonberry bushes. The forward momentum kept us moving, and the rear tires slammed down. The rear bumper dug out a chunk of earth, and we picked up speed on the downward slope. I hit the brakes and steered around a cedar tree, jerked the wheel right to avoid another, bounced hard over a rock, missed another tree, maybe a blue spruce, and came to a jarring halt when the front bumper mated with the stump of a Douglas fir.

Morphy had his front paws splayed out like the support feet on a backhoe. He was panting but unhurt. When I got out to survey the damage, he leapt over the front seat and jumped to the ground like a spooked cat.

"Big baby," I said.

He barked and trotted off to smell the apparently fascinating scents of new territory.

I walked around my car with one hand on the cool metal at all times, like it was a horse and might be startled otherwise. The front bumper had cut fresh white gashes into the top of the stump, but wasn't wedged high enough for the front tires to have come up off the ground. The back bumper was decorated with long weeds that had snagged the corners and been ripped from the ground. Chunks of soil and clumps of grass were packed into the hollow under the bumper like dough stuffed into a mold. Nothing seemed to be leaking, though and there was no real damage.

Behind the car was a flattened swath of destruction that told the tale of my off-road adventure—twisted and broken ferns, bent tree branches, and plowed-up earth. The local squirrel population probably hadn't seen so much action since the tree, on the remainder of which my car rested on, had been cut down.

Morphy barked, and I looked up to find him. He was about twenty yards in front of the Land Cruiser and looking away. When I joined him, I could see what had his attention. It was a small cabin. To my left was a dirt driveway that came down from the road I'd left with such abruptness. I looked back to the car and then up to where I'd driven over the edge. Carla's directions had mentioned a hairpin turn just before Walt's cabin. I patted Morphy on the head. "Good boy, Morph."

Usually when people envision a cabin in the woods, they think of Abraham Lincoln, and a small home built of logs with a big chimney made from stones on one side. At least that's the image my mind came up with. Margie

Kelly had painted a more accurate picture of her husband's cabin with the single word *shack*.

The structure in front of me lacked character. The walls were nothing more than plywood with a coat of red paint. The roof was rusted, corrugated steel and hung about three feet over the walls. Two windows, one on each side of the peeling white door, faced the parking area in front. They were covered from inside with Seattle Seahawks blankets. If it wasn't for the black pickup truck parked outside, I would have thought the place abandoned.

The ground to the front and side of the cabin was bare, but when I made my way far enough into the trees to where I could see the back, there were two tall trashcans spilling over with glass jars, coffee filters, and junk food wrappers. There were several portable propane tanks lying on the ground, and the closer I got to the cabin, the more I became aware of a sharp ammonia smell in the air.

I backtracked and came out into the clearing behind the pickup. There was nothing but a bright blue plastic tarp and a handful of bungee cords in the bed of the truck. The back window was covered with white stick-on letters that spelled out: *Don't mess with bad ass Billy*. Charming. The cab was littered with paper sacks, crumpled aluminum beer cans, and loose change on the floorboard. Lying across the bench seat of the truck was a small boy, maybe three or four years old, fast asleep. He was partially covered with a thin blue blanket that looked like it came from a hospital. A one-eyed teddy bear kept watch from the dashboard.

"Hey! What the hell are you doing to my truck?"

I looked up and saw a man in his late twenties walking toward me, his gaze hard, like he had a purpose. Billy, I presumed.

I stepped back from the truck. "Nothing," I said. "I ran off the road over there and was just coming over to see if I could get some help."

"By lookin' in my truck?" He came to a stop less than an arm's length in front of me, and stood tall. His hair was black and stringy and hung over his face, like a shredded veil. He wore a vintage, olive-colored army shirt buttoned to the top with the sleeves down, matching military-style khakis, and black boots. He looked like a G.I. reject.

"I was just coming up to knock on the door, and looked in," I said.

"Don't lie to me!" he yelled and shoved me backward. His hands had come up fast and I only had time to keep my balance, not deflect.

"Look. I ran off the road. My car's right over there. I just need help getting it off of a stump."

His eyes were wide and his hands balled into fists. He moved forward slowly while I backed up. Not a good situation for me. He wanted to fight, either out of irrational rage, mental illness, or drugs. I wasn't sure which. No matter which it was, he wouldn't be satisfied until he hit me.

It wasn't his size that made me nervous; he was only about six feet and on the thin side of one hundred sixty pounds. It was the look in his eyes. It was angry and flat and told me if he got the upper hand, he wouldn't stop. So I had to ask myself, since I was on the retreat, would an initial attack catch him off guard?

I took one more step back and shifted my weight.

Morphy barked and I turned to see where he was. Big mistake. Part of me said, *Duck!* but the stronger (and dumber) side forced me to look back at Billy.

I turned right into his oncoming fist. The lights blinked, the thin bones that formed my nose crunched, and I fell hard on the packed dirt. Blood spurted and then flowed warm and slick over my lips. I shook my head to try and jumpstart my brain but only succeeded in rattling the bones of my freshly broken nose. Bolts of pain shot through my skull and kept me from getting my bearings.

Morphy was closer and sounded like an entire kennel of pissed off dogs. Somehow I didn't think a guy who left a kid in his truck while he cooked drugs would be an animal lover.

I turned over to push myself up from a hands and knees position, but I wobbled, fighting the heaviness behind my eyes. Before I could stand, Billy gave me a kick to the chest that let me know what a football felt like on its way to a forty-five yard field goal. I rolled away, wanting to put some distance between me and this guy's boot. Morphy had another idea.

My dog leapt over me as I rolled, and planted himself between me and my attacker. His teeth were bared and looked like an enameled steel trap, ropes of saliva hung from his jowls and his hair rose like a stiff bristle brush. Morphy snarled and snapped, growled and barked. I'd never seen him so savage, and Billy took a hesitant step backward.

Morphy advanced confidently and gnashed his teeth in the air with the ferocity of instinctual rage. Then he lunged. Our opponent stumbled back and fell down, landing hard on his hip. Morphy went after the closest flailing leg and chomped down hard on Billy's ankle. Once he had a good grip, Morphy twisted his body and shook his head with as much force as he could. The motion wasn't much, since the ankle in Morphy's mouth was still attached to the owner, but given the amount of screaming Billy did, it seemed to be having the effect Morphy intended.

I crabbed backward, away from the melee, and forced myself up on my feet. My nose throbbed and I was doubled over from the pain in my ribs where I'd been kicked. Two more steps, and I reached the edge of the clearing. "Billy!" I yelled. His eyes narrowed and his gaze shot in my direction. "You might want to take care of your kid. He looks scared."

Billy rolled and twisted until he could see the cab of his truck. The little boy was awake. His hands and face pressed up against the passenger's window. His eyes were white, and the glass was fogged where his mouth gaped open.

When Billy turned back around, his face was confused, surprised even. He must have been sampling the meth he'd been cooking inside the cabin. He'd probably forgotten the boy was in the truck.

Morphy was still locked onto Billy's leg, and his growling gained a second wind. Billy kicked Morphy in the shoulder to dislodge him, and the dog finally gave way.

"Morphy!" I called. "That's enough, boy! Come on!" Morphy looked at me and then back at Billy, who scrambled to stand up. He barked once at his prey, then turned and bounded toward me. Billy limped to the cabin, and I pulled Morphy further into the trees with me. A few seconds later, two gunshots cracked the mountain air and bullets zipped overhead.

I ducked behind a tree and looked for other spots that would offer some cover in case Billy followed me into the woods. Two shots were enough, though. His truck roared to life, and judging by the sound of spitting gravel and whine of the engine, it tore out of the clearing in front of Walt's cabin.

Morphy sat next to me at the base of the tree until the rumbling of Billy's truck faded down the mountainside. He bore a smile as he panted and stared at me. His blond muzzle was flecked with blood, dirt, and saliva. I wiped away as much of the blood as I could, worried the drugs and who-knew-what-else in Billy's system would end up in my dog. Morphy tolerated my mothering for a few seconds before standing up on all fours to lick my face, as if to say I should worry about my own blood.

I scratched and pulled his ears gently and gave him a hug. "Good boy, Morphy. Good boy."

18

Morphy and I picked our way through the underbrush back to the cabin. A padlock secured the front door of Walt and Margie's little shack. As bad as I wanted to kick in the door or smash a window to get inside, it wouldn't do any good. Without a camera to take photographs of what I found, there was no point to it. There was enough evidence outside anyway to give the police probable cause.

I got a closer look of the barrels around back, which were crammed with empty bottles, jars with burn marks, cans of paint thinner, bags of rock salt, and lots of broken glass, and they had that burning ammonia smell. Everything I'd learned from Jason Minor and the few websites I'd visited on Brian Kelly's computer told me all of the odors and garbage around the cabin were signs of a meth lab. The glassware was used in cooking it, and the odor was a byproduct.

In the clearing, I found what was left of my cell phone. In the scuffle, it must have fallen off my belt. It had been reduced to nothing more than useless plastic pieces and tiny metal screws ready for the recycling heap. I checked my hip pockets and inside my jacket only to discover my wallet was missing. I glanced around the clearing, and saw it lying like a dead bird with its wings spread open. I picked it up and found my driver's license and cash missing. Fantastic.

I walked back to the car and called to Morphy. My body throbbed to the beat of my pulse, it was getting cold, and I was hungry. I checked my face in the side view mirror of my car and wiped away a bloody beard with the sleeve of my jacket. My nose was crooked. I braced myself against the car door before I shoved it back into place. I muffled a cry of agony but then let it out, hearing it echo among the trees. Who cared what the squirrels thought?

There was no way I would make my date with Carla. I needed to find a phone. Morphy jumped into the back of the Land Cruiser and lay flat on the floor. Once I was strapped in, I turned over the engine, locked in the four-wheel drive, dropped the shifter into reverse, and floored the gas. The engine revved, and then with a screech of metal, the car jumped backward off of the stump. It sounded like a cork being popped from a paper champagne bottle.

I got back out to inspect the front end of my car. The fiberglass shell around the bumper was torn away. I picked up the long piece of plastic and tossed it into the back with Morphy. In the gloomy light, it was hard to tell if any metal was twisted or if any fluids had leaked. Not that it mattered. I was going to leave anyway.

I maneuvered the Land Cruiser around the stump and into the clearing in front of the cabin. So far, so good, the car still ran. At the top of the small driveway, I discovered why Billy was surprised to see me. Stretched across the entry was a chain suspended by a small pole at each end, and on the chain was a sign: *Danger Do Not Enter — Biohazard.*

The chain was the thin type used to keep a dog tethered, not the heavy gauge steel a state facility would use. But with a sign like that, the last thing a person would do was wonder about the chain. I stomped on the gas and broke through the barrier. Trespassing laws be damned. I was breaking out, not in.

Once I wound my way back out to Highway 12, I put in an hour of slow driving and arrived unscathed in Packwood, a small lumber community doomed to become the Pompeii of the United States should Mt. Rainier ever decide to erupt. I pulled into a gas station on the edge of town and called Carla from a payphone.

"You're not coming, are you?" she said.

"I ran into a little trouble. I'm on my way, but I'm going to be late."

"A little trouble?"

"Well, a fist actually."

"What? Ray, what is going on?"

"It's a long story and I'll tell you everything, but I need to call the police first."

"The police? Ray…!"

"Okay," I said. "Four words. Bad guy and meth lab. I'll call you when I get there."

I hung up the phone and turned around to wave at Morphy. He sat up watching me through the window, oblivious to the black 4x4 truck at the service island behind him. Billy sat behind the wheel staring into the darkness in front of him.

I walked across the asphalt with my eye on Billy. The little boy I'd seen sleeping earlier leaned forward and observed me from behind his daddy's shoulder. Had they followed me or was our convergence just bad luck?

"That's an ugly face you got there, Ray." Billy said and turned to look at me. He held up my driver's license. He knew my name and where I lived. "Hope you didn't just call the cops. That would be bad."

"For who?" I came to a stop by my driver's side door. "You or me? Will your boss be mad? What will he do?"

He looked back out his windshield, then at me. "Who says I got a boss?"

"Your hesitation for one. It's amazing how much someone says without saying anything at all. I also happen to know who owns that cabin, and it's not you."

"Yeah? Well I'm just sayin' you better not have called the cops. You gettin' laid out like that was your own fault."

"Mmm hmm." I got into the Land Cruiser and started it up. "Hey, is the food over there any good?" I pointed to a little restaurant on the other side of the gas station. Billy ignored me and looked out his windshield again. "No comment? Okay. I guess I'll just have to try it myself, then."

I pulled out of the gas station and slowly turned a wide U to park in front of the eatery. I didn't need to look over my shoulder to know I was being watched as I walked inside and took a window seat.

A waitress, with a plastic nameplate that labeled her as "Betty," wearing a powder blue uniform straight out of the nineteen fifties, stopped just short of my table and passed me a menu. Her upper lip curled like a wave and she said, "Honey, are you okay?"

"It's not as bad as it looks." I took the menu from her and scanned the specials.

"It looks like you got your nose broke and haven't had the opportunity to clean it up."

"Oh. I guess it's exactly what it looks like." I smiled weakly and glanced out the window. "Where are your restrooms?"

She pointed to a hallway by the kitchen, and then retreated to check on her other customers.

When the bell above the door behind me tinkled, I didn't need to look in order to know it was Billy. His lanky form strutted by, and he sat two booths down, facing my direction.

I stood up. "Order me a burger when she comes back, will ya?" I said to him. "I'm going to go wash up."

Billy didn't say anything, and I ducked a taxidermy monument to a bull elk on my way down the hallway.

In the bathroom, I rinsed my face with cold water and used a damp paper towel to wipe away the blood I'd only succeeded in smearing all over myself up in the mountains. I worked quickly and avoided the bridge of my nose altogether. When I was done, I moved out to the hallway quietly, checked to make sure Billy wasn't looking for me, then walked around the corner into the kitchen and out the back door. I had no idea where I would end up, but if I asked someone, it might appear as if I didn't belong. Once outside, I stopped to get my bearings, then slid along the wall until I could see the parking lot.

Billy's truck had a set of big tires called "mudders" for off-roading. They were thick, and the heavy tread made a coarse humming sound when driven on pavement. I unscrewed the cap to the air stem of the rear driver's side tire of Billy's truck and leaned my thumbnail into it, letting the air out. Two cars went by on the street, but neither honked or turned around to confront me. I pushed harder. Billy wouldn't have the patience to wait too long. He'd go into the bathroom sooner or later to see what I was up to.

I chanced a look into the restaurant and saw Billy on his feet, his menacing stride taking him toward the restrooms. I ducked back down next to the now leaning truck. The rushing air slowed down as the tire flattened against the asphalt. Then Morphy and I bid adieu to the city of Packwood with smiles on our faces.

19

■ The smiles didn't last long. Morphy fell asleep after fifteen minutes, and my nose began to bleed again until I staunched it with a paper napkin smeared with taco sauce from our quick meal earlier.

As I drove through the evening, I could think of little else but Billy and Brian Kelly. My first thought was they knew each other from college, but Billy was young enough that he and Brian wouldn't have attended together. So how had they met? Through the veterinary clinic? A football game? Jail? I made a mental note to check if Brian Kelly had a criminal record, and drove on.

I followed Highway 12 until it connected with I-5 and headed north. It was a long way to go, and I knew there must be shorter routes, but I wasn't familiar with the area and just wanted to get home.

Just after nine p.m., the twinkling lights of the Seattle skyline came into view and brought the night to life. I felt better just knowing the comfort of my bed awaited. The water on Elliot Bay was surprisingly smooth, and when I rolled down the window, Morphy sat up to smell the cool air mixed with sea salt, industry, and a touch of diesel exhaust.

At the bottom of Dravus Street, I stopped at Red Mill Burgers and ordered two cheeseburgers to go. While those were cooking, I stepped outside and called Carla from a payphone.

"I thought you said you were going to be late, not *late*," she said when I told her who it was.

"Sorry. How about you come over and I'll make you a burger."

"By 'make me a burger,' do you mean Red Mill?"

"Of course."

"Where are you?"

"I'm here now. Already ordered."

"I'm on my way."

It would take Carla about half an hour to get to my place. I had a small house in the Magnolia area of Seattle, with nice views of downtown to the south and Puget Sound to the west. During the winter, I watched heavy clouds wrestle around the Olympic Mountains then sneak over the water to hide the Space Needle in fog. Summer months were filled with sparkling sunsets, passenger-heavy ferryboats, and the occasional lightning storm.

When Carla arrived at the front door, Morphy and I had been home less than five minutes, and the burgers were still hot. "How many laws did you break to get here so fast?" I asked.

"Glad to see you, too." She smiled. "Besides, it doesn't matter if I was speeding. It's a Red Mill burger. Any cop would have understood."

She was probably right about that. Everyone knew Red Mill burgers were the best in Seattle, and it would be a bigger crime to let one go to waste.

We moved into the living room where I'd left the food and I asked her if she wanted beer or wine. "Ray," she said, "no one drinks wine with—Oh, my God! What happened to your face?"

"I told you I ran into a little trouble."

I touched lightly between my blackening eyes. My skin felt like an orange peel. When I looked in the mirror, I saw the bruising was worse, and blood was smeared over my upper lip again. No wonder I'd gotten wide-eyed looks from restaurant folks all night.

Carla dragged me into the bathroom, where she pushed me down on the toilet, started some warm water running in the sink, and then rummaged through the drawers and medicine cabinet. "How long has it been like this?" she asked.

"I don't know." I shrugged. "Since it happened this afternoon."

"Why didn't you take care of it? Do you know what this is going to look like at the wedding?"

The wedding. I'd forgotten about the wedding. "Who are these people again?"

Carla rolled her eyes and dabbed a warm washcloth under my nose. "I told you. Angie works in the Treasurer's Department at the Court House. Her fiancé is Aaron Atkinson."

"Angie and Aaron Atkinson? Will they name their kids Amber and Allan?"

"I have no idea, Ray. Now hold still. This is going to be hard to disguise."

"What do you mean disguise?"

"If the swelling goes down enough, we can put some foundation on it to hide the bruising."

"I am *not* wearing make-up. If anyone asks, I'll just say the bachelor party got out of hand."

Carla finished her nursing by sticking a butterfly bandage over my nose with enough pressure to make my eyes water, which meant there was no way I was going to the wedding without hiding my injuries. "There. It already looks better. Now, how about that dinner?"

We stopped at the refrigerator for two beers, then sat on the floor of the living room to eat on the coffee table. I brought Carla up to speed on what I had been doing in Yakima and my concerns about Walter Kelly's death.

"You really think his own son would kill him over a shack in the woods?"

"Depends on how much the property is worth or if he's using it as a drug factory. People have killed for less. Besides, whatever they're making up there might be bringing in a pretty penny, too."

"Kind of a gruesome way to kill your dad."

"I know."

"Do you think the guy at the cabin will come after you here?" she asked, her voice soft.

I shook my head. "No reason to. I didn't really see anything, and no cop is going to go up there looking for a jerk who punched me."

But I wasn't sure if I believed it myself. Billy seemed the type to pack a grudge around with him for years, and I'm sure I'd poked his anti-social psychosis a bit by flattening his tire and escaping from Packwood. I made a mental note to double-check the locks before going to bed.

"Hey, where's my package?" I asked, partly to change the subject.

"What package?"

A quick scare rolled through me, like once when I'd thought my car had been stolen, only to realize I'd parked it in a different spot than I remembered. A handmade chessboard crafted by Walter Kelly was not something I wanted to lose. It wasn't Walt's status as a demigod of the woodworking world that gave the chessboard its worth, but the sentimental value. My friendship with Walt—along with his connection to my mother, although remote and ancient—was what made it special. That, and the fact that it was a chessboard. "What package?" I said. "Carla, I told you on the phone I thought there should be a big package here at the house, and I asked you to pick it up for me."

"Oh, that." She waved her hand. "I couldn't get it right away, so I asked my mom to do it."

"Your mom? Why?"

"You wanted it picked up. It's picked up. What's the big deal?"

I looked at the clock on the wall. "We need to go get it."

"Now?"

"Yes. Now."

"Ray, you're crazy. What's in it?"

"A chessboard, I think."

"You have twenty chessboards!"

"Carla. Please. I know I'm nuts, but I'd really like to go and get it. And I don't have twenty chessboards. I have twelve."

"Okay," she said. "Okay, we'll go get it."

We cleaned up the mess on the coffee table and went outside to Carla's car. Morphy'd had enough riding around for one day, and decided to call it a night on the living room couch.

"You don't suppose your mom checked my mail, do you?" I asked.

"She doesn't know you. Why would she?"

"I better check it. Hold on."

I trotted up to the curb and opened my mailbox. As Carla backed her car up the driveway to meet me, my day (while pretty much over at ten p.m.) got a whole lot better. Amidst the junk mail were three postcards with moves from correspondence chess games.

20

■ Carla Caplicki's mother lived in a two-story colonial with an immaculately maintained yard. The hedges near the sidewalk and halfway up the drive were neatly rounded with no stray twigs or leaves. A row of knee-high lights illuminated the walk to the front door and also revealed the manicured lawn and weedless flowerbeds. The front steps and the porch were covered with rough, grass-colored indoor/outdoor carpeting, and were well-lit by a single, large chandelier that reminded me of the one at the White House.

Carla looked at her watch and rang the bell. "It's after ten thirty," she whispered. "I don't know if she's awake." There were a couple of lights burning somewhere in the house, but Carla said her mother left them on for appearances.

"Appearances?" I asked.

"You know, for safety. It makes people think she's awake."

The light behind the front door popped on, and I saw blurred movement behind the small pane of textured glass set in the door. "Who is it, please?" came a woman's voice. I'd expected a demure little-old-lady's voice, but Carla's mother had a commanding tone that expected an answer.

"It's me, Mom," Carla said.

There were two *clicks* and a rattle of chain as locks opened and then the door swung inward. I'd pictured Carla's mother as an immigrant from the early nineteen hundreds, stout and wrinkly and wearing a black babushka. Instead Mrs. Caplicki stood about five foot nine, had a flowing mane of recently brushed black hair, and wore silvery silk pajamas beneath a billowy robe of the same sheen. "It's a little late, honey, but you and your friend can come in."

Carla stepped across the threshold. I followed her past her mother and into the living room, where we stood in front of a stiff-looking flowery couch.

"Introduce me to this handsome young man, Carla," her mother said.

"This is Ray. Ray Gordon. We went to high school together."

"Oh, yes. Ray Gordon. I've heard about you." Mrs. Caplicki smiled and I thought she winked, but it might have just been that I was exhausted. "Why has it taken so long for us to meet?"

"I'm not sure," I said. "I get nervous around pretty women."

"Oh, a charmer!" She waved away the comment like she heard it every day. "What happened to your face, Ray?"

"Carla hit me," I said.

Carla's elbow shot out and struck me in the ribs. "Mom, remember when I asked you to go to a house and pick up a package?"

"Is that why you're here?"

"Yes, Ray's insane."

"Oh, I doubt that."

"No, it's true," I said.

Mrs. Caplicki laughed. "Why don't you two have a seat and I'll go and get it."

Carla and I sat on the edge of the flowery couch with our backs straight and our knees together. We looked like two nervous teenagers about to go to the prom. "You didn't tell me your mom was hot," I whispered to Carla. Her elbow flew back again and connected with my stomach.

When Mrs. Caplicki returned, she carried a box big enough for a really thick, extra-large pizza. "Here it is, Ray." She handed it to me reverently. "It must be very important." I looked at her wondering why she would say such a thing. "Well, it is the middle of the night," she said, obviously reading the expression on my face.

"Some people probably think it's not important—" I glanced toward Carla "—but it's very important to me. A friend of mine made this for me before he died."

"I see. What is it, if you don't mind my asking?"

"It's a chessboard." I set the package on the coffee table and smoothed my hands over the wide, flat surface.

"Open it up, Ray," Carla said.

Mrs. Caplicki sat in a chair on the other side of the coffee table. "Yes. Let's see it."

I used a ballpoint pen to poke a few holes in the packaging tape, and then tore the tape apart where it kept the box flaps closed. Carla stood up, holding the carton while I pulled out the bubble-wrapped contents, and then set it aside so the coffee table was clear. I unfolded the plastic and found another protective layer beneath it. Carla took the bubble wrap and started squeezing until the room was filled with the sound of popping. Mrs. Caplicki and I both looked at Carla until she stopped.

"Oh, come on," Carla said. "Neither of you can tell me you don't like to pop bubble wrap. Everybody likes to pop bubble wrap."

I pulled away the second layer, like a sculptor unveiling his art, revealing the chessboard beneath. The board was exactly that, a work of art, and it caught my breath. The dark squares were almost black, probably made of ebony, and the light squares had a subtle grain that created an illusion of movement.

The frame was also a dark wood, but not as dense as the squares of the playing surface. It was beveled and the edges sloped down, away from the top, and had a slight cove all the way around. At each corner was a carved claw holding a ball, similar to antique table legs. While the claws were part of the frame, they appeared to be holding the board up all by themselves.

The checkered field of sixty-four squares was raised slightly, maybe a quarter of an inch, above the frame, and the edges were rounded over just enough to take off the sharpness. Each square looked to be about two and a quarter inches—my favorite size for a playing board—and the frame was about two inches wide.

I ran my hands over the lacquered, glass-like playing surface, the carved claw-foot corners, and the coved frame. I sat back and shook my head.

"It's beautiful," Mrs. Caplicki said.

"Wow," Carla said. "It really is. Ray, it's gorgeous."

"I've never seen a board like it. How could he have known? Look at this wood. It's…" I trailed off, unable to finish my thought.

"What, Ray?" Carla put her hand in mine, and I squeezed her fingers.

"I was going to say I wish I could thank him. And I just figured out how I can."

"What?" Carla glanced at her mother. "Ray, Walter's gone. You can't thank him."

"Oh, yes I can." I pulled the two postcards I'd retrieved from my mailbox out of my jacket pocket and held them up. "I've got three correspondence games right here and a beautiful new chessboard to play them on."

"Ray, it's getting late," Carla said.

"I know. We better get going."

21

■ Carla wasn't as enthusiastic as I was about trying out my new chessboard as soon as we got back to my house. In truth, I was beginning to fade the closer to home we got. The last time I'd gotten up at five thirty a.m. was for a paper route I'd had when I was fifteen. Besides, the mental energy I'd expended searching libraries and illegally-obtained computer information, plus the quick meeting with Billy's fist, had my body about ready to go on strike. My eyes were slow and my brain thick.

Once we got inside my house, I set the chessboard on the coffee table and asked Carla to sit down. "Do you want a nightcap?"

"Ray, it's almost midnight, and I need to work tomorrow."

"I'm not going to play through the correspondence games. I just want to set the board up and see how my nice pieces look on it."

"Which is your *nice* set? You have about fifty."

"You know I don't have fifty sets of chess pieces. Yet."

She rolled her eyes.

Actually, I only have about twenty different sets of chess pieces, which to some might seem extravagant, but I know plenty of people with more. We call it collecting, while others (like Carla) call it craziness.

Some of the sets were plastic, some wood, some even cast in metal or carved from stone. My favorite and best set was rosewood, carved in the classic Staunton style. It had a nice weight to it, and delivered a resonant *thump* when the pieces were picked up and moved from square to square.

Carla sat down on the sofa. I went into the kitchen to fix us each a drink, but decided to open a bottle of wine. It took me only a minute or two to pull the cork and pour two glasses, but when I reentered the living room, Carla was in tears.

"Carla—" I put the glasses on the table "—what's wrong?"

"Ray, I'm so sorry. You don't have to go to the wedding if you don't want to."

"What are you talking about? What happened?"

She choked back a sob and pointed at the chessboard. I followed the line of her finger to the corner of the frame and a twisted ball and claw. "I broke your chessboard!" she wailed.

I sat on the floor across the table from her and rotated the board to bring the corner in question in front of me. The small claw holding the ball was twisted about forty-five degrees to the left. The chessboard didn't seem to be off balance, though. It sat on the table solidly without tipping.

"What exactly did you do?"

She sniffed and wiped a black smear of mascara under her eyes. "I was just looking at it, running my finger over the carving, and it moved. I thought I was just seeing things because I'm so tired. I pushed harder and it turned all the way over like that. I'm sorry, Ray!"

I twisted the claw back down to match the others. It seemed loose, but when I tried to rotate the other carved feet, they wouldn't budge. I came back to the broken one and turned it all the way around.

"They're probably just glued in, Carla," I said. "It probably just came loose during shipping."

With my thumb and index finger, I pulled the claw, expecting it to pop right out with maybe a one-inch plug sticking out the back of it. Instead, the dowel grew longer, and when it emerged, it was about as long as a drinking straw and the diameter of a nickel. "What in the world? I'm no expert, but this seems a bit excessive, don't you think?"

Carla nodded and then pointed to the end of it. "It's hollow." She scooted to the edge of the sofa in order to see better.

I turned it over to look for myself. Not only was the dowel hollow, there was a scrap of paper curled up inside. "Do you have a pair of tweezers on you?" I asked Carla.

She opened her purse and rummaged through it. Her face was almost inside the bag as she pushed flotsam to one side, then the other. Finally shoving her arm in up to her elbow, she fished a bit more, then pulled out the elusive little tool. She handed them to me triumphantly and smiled.

"What else do you have in there?" I asked.

"Nothing you need to worry about."

"This doesn't make up for breaking my chessboard." Her smile fell and I laughed. "I'm just kidding. I don't think you broke it at all. I think you found a secret compartment."

I took a deep breath, summoned up any and all skill I may have acquired as a child while playing the Operation game, and reached into the tube with Carla's tweezers. I grasped the paper and slowly tugged it out.

Unrolled, the scrap of paper turned out to be a photograph of a bunch of teenagers in what appeared to be a high school pep band. The picture was black-and-white, sported a few thin creases across the corners, and featured a white border. It was the kind of photo a student photographer would take for a school newspaper or yearbook.

"Who are they?" Carla asked.

"I don't know about the rest of them, but she—" I pointed "—is my mom."

"Oh, my God, Ray! Really?"

I nodded. She was obviously younger, her hair was longer than I'd ever seen it, but there was no doubt.

"You have her eyes," Carla said.

I nodded again and stood up. I felt like a walnut was wedged in my throat. "More wine?" I walked into the kitchen without waiting for an answer. I uncorked the merlot and swallowed two gulps straight from the bottle to wash down the lump.

"Are you okay?" Carla asked from behind me in the doorway. I turned around and nodded, but my traitorous eyes teared up.

Carla stepped closer and pulled me to her. She held me tight and didn't say a word when I choked out a sob of my own.

"I'm sorry," I said and pulled away. I grabbed the kitchen towel from the stove handle and wiped my face with it. "I really don't know what's wrong with me. You'd think I'd be happy to see a picture like that."

"Ray, you and I have known each other almost our entire lives. In all that time, I think you've never really known who you are. Tonight, you got a glimpse. I'm sure it's a little overwhelming."

"Maybe," I said. My mother had been a different person when that picture was taken. The furthest thing from her mind was a child—me. Not that that was a bad thing. She couldn't have been more than fifteen or sixteen years old at the time. She'd been a musician. When I was that age, I was in a chess club.

"Hey, come here." I took hold of Carla's hand and led her back into the living room. She sat on the sofa, while I found one of my high school yearbooks and pulled it off the shelf. I sat next to Carla and flipped the pages until I found the photo I wanted.

"Oh, my gosh, Ray. Look at that."

The two pictures, the one Walt sent me and the one in my yearbook, were probably separated by two decades yet were almost identical. Not in a mystical, lost universe sort of way, but in that goofy, teenager, posed-picture sort of way on display in every yearbook everywhere, at least since the flashbulb was invented and people didn't have to remain rigid during a photo shoot.

What struck me was how my then-teenaged mother and the then-teenaged me were posed the same way — it was like looking into a mirror and seeing someone who was me but not quite. We both had a crooked smile that leaned slightly to the right, each of us stood on one leg at the end of the group while a friend held the other leg up at a right angle. The clothing was different, the hairstyles laughable, and she brandished a flute while I held chess pieces between my fingers. And Carla was right. That was my mom in the picture, and it gave me a tiny but remarkable glimpse into who I was.

"That's pretty neat, Ray. I wonder how Walt got hold of it."

"I don't know. Maybe he was the school photographer, or he knew someone who was."

"That's a very special gift."

I knew it was, but I didn't want to talk anymore about it. At least not right then. There was no reason to risk another outburst of emotion in front of Carla. I just didn't say anything.

"Now what?" she asked.

I smiled weakly. "I'm pretty tired."

"Then I suggest you go to bed." Carla stood up and stretched, arching her back like a cat, and yawned. Her shirt pulled up to expose her midriff and I was drawn to her bared skin. I felt vaguely naughty, like when I was a kid and spied on my teenaged neighbor sunbathing in a bikini. I started to study the chessboard before Carla caught me looking. "I need to get some sleep myself," she said. "I have to go in to work early, so I can get my dress refitted."

"What dress?"

"Ray. So help me, if you forget about the wedding, I'll shove that secret compartment right up your broken nose."

I laughed. The mood had certainly changed. "Don't worry. You're still going to come with me to get my tux, right?"

"Of course. If I don't, you'll get the wrong color cummerbund."

"Goodnight, Carla."

"G'night. See you tomorrow." She gave Morphy a neck rub. At the door, she blew me a kiss, then went out into the night.

I picked up the picture of my mother and her high school band. She'd played the flute, and I'd never known. The lump returned to my throat. I closed the picture between the pages of my yearbook and set it aside.

I poured more wine, then brought the chessboard over by the wall, to a small table I used just for chess. My various sets of pieces were stashed around the house, some bagged in the closet, and others in boxes on shelves or under the bed. I pulled my favorite wood pieces from the bookshelf and set them up on the board.

The dark pieces were rosewood with a thick grain, and the light pieces, like almost all light wooden chess pieces, were carved from boxwood.

Wood chessmen give the game a more seductive feel than plastic, but the important thing is weight. If the King or Rook, or any other piece for that matter, doesn't have enough heft to provide authority when moved from square to square, the mystery and art of chess vanish.

Once I had the pieces set up, I decided the rosewood clashed with the dark wood Walt had used for the chessboard. None of my other sets would do, either. Right then and there, I made up my mind to shop for a set of chessmen to suit the board. In the meantime, I decided to break in this gift Walt had given me by seeing if I could discover why he had a problem with the Evergreen Game.

The opening moves were nothing extraordinary. The King's pawns came out to the center, a Knight and Bishop from each side entered the game, and then White advanced the b pawn. With each move, I stared at the board and tried to see a position that might lead me to discover what problem Walt had been having. But nothing jumped out. My head would fall forward every so often under the weight of my exhaustion. I looked at Morphy, who was curled up on the sofa under the window. I thought he had the right idea. Then the pieces would capture my attention again, and I went back to the battle being played out on the board.

On the twelfth move, things began to look maybe a little tougher for someone to see, but I still didn't think of it as a "problem." White's Bishops were both poised to attack Black's kingside, the Rook on e1 was aimed right up the middle, and the Queen was focused on the center of the board as well as the enemy King.

BLACK

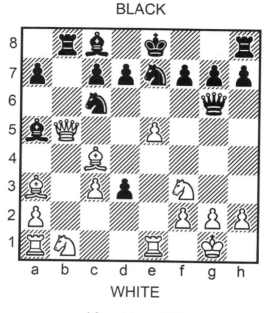

WHITE

After 12. ...Rb8

Black, on the other hand, had left his King in the center instead of castling to safety, and his Queen was on an unusual square. From where it was placed, the Black Queen threatened nothing. And though his Rook on b8 was attacking the White Queen, it was an empty threat. All White needed to do was move the Queen to safety on a4, where she still eyed the same areas as before.

At move nineteen, after White lost both Knights, I thought maybe this was where Walt had lost his way, but my head was too clogged with fatigue to really focus. While the position was recognizable to me, it might have been like trying to find a way through a foggy forest for Walt. The trees were familiar, but through the mist, they all looked the same, and he could easily be walking in circles.

I staggered through the remaining moves. When I reached the final position, I smiled and really understood why it was called the Evergreen Game.

Very often in modern chess, the games between grandmasters and other brilliant players ended in draws or resignations. The game Walt was studying ended in checkmate—and a spectacular one at that. Not only did White sacrifice a lot of his pieces—including the Queen— to achieve the final position he was after, but he was only one move away from losing the game himself.

BLACK

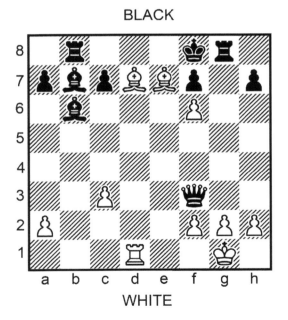

WHITE

Final position after 24. Bxe7 Checkmate

I sat back in my chair and laughed. It was an old game, played long before Bobby Fischer's heyday in the nineteen sixties and early seventies, but it still held the imagination.

I rubbed my eyes and looked at the clock. Just shy of two a.m.

22

■ The following morning, with a cup of coffee in hand and while Morphy was outside taking care of business, I wondered what might have happened last night with Carla. Maybe it was time for me to either face up to a real relationship, or go see a shrink.

I sat in front of the chessboard and double-checked to see if the other ball-and-claw carvings at the corners were removable, as well. I nudged, pushed, prodded, and twisted, but they wouldn't budge, so I quit trying for fear of breaking them. I sighed and nodded. No more pictures.

With the coffee pot drained, I decided to let photo memories go for the moment and concentrate on the unpleasant task at hand: tuxedo rental. After the people Carla worked with at the King County Courthouse told me she hadn't shown up for work, I called her at home. Carla didn't answer there, either. I was just about to decide whether I should start to worry, or if she was just playing hooky from work to get her final dress fitting early, when the phone rang.

"Carla," I said, thinking she'd caller ID'd me, "I thought you…"

"Sorry, lover boy," a distinctly male voice sneered, "your girlfriend can't talk right now."

"Who is this?"

"Oh, I think you'll figure it out," he said. "But I'll give you a hint. My tires are very expensive."

My face flushed in anger. "Billy," I said evenly, "it's great to hear from you."

"See? Sometimes you can be smart. Too bad you weren't last night."

"What do you want?"

"I got what I want. For now. When I'm done playin' with her, I'll come get you. Then we'll find out what I need to do next."

Did he really have Carla? I wondered in a panic. Was he insane enough to kidnap her? Or was he bluffing? "You like picking on girls?" I asked, faking a laugh and hoping I didn't sound rattled. Billy seemed like the bully type, someone that playground psychology would work on. "You too afraid of someone who'll hit back?"

"You didn't hit back, Gordon. Or don't you remember? Oh, that's right. You went down after one little smack." He laughed.

"Cheap shot. If the only way you can win a fight is to cheat, then maybe a girl is your best opponent."

Billy breathed deeply and sighed into the phone. "Just when I thought you were gettin' smart, you go and say somethin' stupid like that. Keep it up and you'll likely get killed."

"Is that a threat?"

"You bet your ass it is."

There was no doubt in my mind Billy would follow through on whatever violence he promised. I would much rather he bring it to me than take it out on Carla, though. "Well, try this for a threat," I said. "If you even breathe on her —"

"Ooh. I'm scared, Gordon. I take what I want, when I want it. If you don't like it, then go —"

"Yeah, Billy. You're a real man. I got it. What do you want, huh? Why did you call me? Do you want me to pay for a new tire?"

"I want to know what you were doin' at the cabin yesterday. But I'm not gonna play on your turf, Gordon. I'm going home." There was a beep as he disconnected, and the phone went dead.

23

■ The smart thing to do would have been to call the cops. The problem was, which cops to call? There were the Seattle City Police, the King County Sheriff, or their counterparts in Yakima. I had to assume Billy had snatched Carla after she left my house the night before, which meant he could have been anywhere. He was probably still in Seattle, but asking the police to keep an eye out for a black 4x4 pickup in the state of Washington would be like asking a librarian if she knew of a book with a black cover. They were everywhere! Since I hadn't thought to write down the license plate number of Billy's truck, and didn't know his last name, I really would look like a fool if I called the police.

It was a two-and-a-half-hour drive to Yakima if the traffic was light. If Billy was still in Seattle when he called, it was probably from Carla's house. He would have needed a place to crash, and had either forced her to tell him where she lived, or robbed her of her wallet to find out. A quick trip to her place in morning traffic would give him a lead of about an hour, but I needed to make sure Billy hadn't left Carla for dead.

Morphy and I arrived at Carla's house within forty-five minutes of the phone call from Billy, and pulled into the driveway behind her red Subaru. The black 4x4 was nowhere in sight, but I still moved cautiously around the house, with my attention on the windows, while Morphy sniffed around back. Carla didn't have pets, not even a fish in a bowl, which meant any movement of the curtains would tell me someone was inside.

When I reached the front door, I rang the bell, but no one came to answer. The same results were achieved at the back door. I'd already made up my mind to break a window, but as close as the neighboring houses were, I'd have to do it with more than a little discretion. Once inside, I would only have a few minutes to check the rooms for Carla before someone reported a break-in.

I was looking around the back stoop for something to muffle the sound of breaking glass when I heard a neighbor's door open. I turned to face a woman in her thirties or forties, wearing jeans, a black sweater, and thick gray socks. Her hair was blond and pulled into a ponytail. In one hand, she held a cell phone, in the other, an iron skillet.

"I already dialed 9-1-1." Her thumb was poised over the keypad of the phone, ready to hit the call button. "So are you over there to see someone, steal something, or find your dog?"

Morphy sat at the foot of the stoop with a big smile on his face as he glanced from me to the neighbor. "See someone?" I tried.

"Who?"

"Carla Caplicki. She works for the county, about yea tall, great smile, and likes to say 'bullcrapaloni.'"

The woman laughed and lowered the skillet. "And you are who, exactly?"

"Ray Gordon. Do you know where Carla is?"

She shook her head. "She isn't home, though. I know that. She left this morning with some guy."

"Black truck?" I asked.

"Yeah."

"Was there a little boy?"

"Yeah. Carla was carrying him, like the guy was forcing her to baby-sit or something." Probably not too far from the truth, I thought. "The guy didn't look her type, either," the neighbor said.

"In what way?"

"Kind of scary looking. Long hair, skuzzy clothes, pushy. I think you're more her type." She said, glancing at her toes.

"What makes you say that?"

"Let's just say I recognize your name."

Even under the circumstances, I had to smile. I never thought I'd be reminded of a possible romance by a total stranger while Carla was the victim of kidnapping.

I penned my name and home phone number (since my cell phone was broken) on the back of a gas receipt I found in my glove box and handed it to Carla's neighbor. "If you see or hear anything, please call and leave a message."

She nodded and her ponytail bounced. "Is Carla okay?"

"I hope so."

Washington is one of the few states to possess drastically differing climates. To the west is the Pacific Ocean with miles of rocky shoreline and smooth sand beaches. The Olympic Mountains on the peninsula help block rain clouds, and have one of the only temperate rainforests in North America at their feet. On the other side of Puget Sound, the Cascade Mountain range, with its volcanic jewels, divides the state into east and west. At least according to the politicians. For people who drive I-90, the separation of eastern and western Washington is somewhere between the two small towns of Cle Elum and Ellensburg.

The towering trees blanketing the mountains follow drivers into the foothills and then peter out, like a gravel road devolving into a dirt path. Almost before you can blink, the trees disappear, to be replaced with dusty hills of scrubland, dotted in the valleys with squares of green lawns surrounding ranch houses. Apparently, Washington's motto, "The Evergreen State," only pertains to the western half.

The central Washington desert continues eastward with scabs of rock, veined with mighty rivers until rising up again and changing into rolling farmland, where the wind ripples the wheat and barley in shimmering waves until they flow into Idaho.

In the middle of it all is Ellensburg, where I-84 turns south. The highway is a gray, serpentine scar winding through sage-infested hills populated by rattlesnakes, shiny black beetles, and an occasional scruffy coyote.

Yakima is an oasis in the desert, nestled in a valley where rivers converge and some of the world's most perfect fruit is harvested. All kinds of produce, from apples to zucchini, are grown on farms all the way down to the Columbia River. There are even several wineries that give Napa Valley a reason to worry about its status as the best in the country.

Once I got to Yakima, I didn't drive directly to Margie Kelly's house. If her son Brian showed up or was already there, I didn't want to create a scene. Margie had gone through enough turmoil with the death of her husband, I didn't want to force her to deal with the possibility of her son and daughter-in-law being drug manufacturers as well.

What I needed to do was figure out Billy's last name and where he lived. I'd have to keep an eye on Brian Kelly and see if Billy contacted him. I needed Billy to make a move and come out in the open.

I checked into a motel that accepted pets and told Morphy to choose one of the two queen-sized beds in our room. He leapt onto the one by the window and lay down. I dropped my duffel bag on the other bed and scoped out the room. It was nothing fancy, just the two beds, an old television set atop a battered dresser, a writing table near the window, and a leaning chair. The bathroom was decorated in creamy vinyl, and had porcelain fixtures that looked like they'd been begging to be replaced since the nineteen fifties.

I took a plastic bowl from my bag and filled it with water for Morphy. He lumbered off the bed, lapped at the water, and then rolled over onto his back. "Sorry, pal. I need to go out for a while. I'll give you a good scratching after dinner."

I stepped outside and scanned the street in front of the motel. Phone booths had no place in the world of cellular technology and were becoming harder to find all the time. Using the phone in my room was out of the question. Though I doubted Billy would be smart enough to decipher where I called from, his "employer" Brian Kelly might. Either way, I needed to call Carla's cell phone to make sure she was okay. Billy had probably called me using her phone and not his (if he even had one of his own). Whether I spoke to Carla or Billy, I would find out his next move and draw him out.

Two blocks from the motel, I found what I'd been looking for outside of a Mexican grocery outlet. It wasn't a phone booth so much as a stall I leaned into. I wiped the earpiece on my jeans and punched in Carla's number using my calling card. After three rings, someone answered but didn't say anything.

"Hello?" I said.

"Ray?" It was Carla's voice, shaky and quiet.

"Carla, are you okay?"

"Ray, there's a little boy, but I don't know —"

"Well, well," Billy's voice came on the line. "Hello, Ray. How the hell are you?" He sounded, not…happy, but uplifted, and his speech was slurred. I imagined his eyes were as droopy as his voice.

"You're high, aren't you? That's why you ran home. You needed a fix."

"Best stuff in the world, man."

"Same stuff you're cooking up in the mountains?"

"You know it. It's got a kick, too."

"Where are you, Billy? How about I come over, pay for a new set of tires, and take Carla home. We'll be even, okay?"

He started laughing until he choked and coughed. "I'm not in the mood, Gordon. I want to have some fun first, then I'll come get you. Just be patient."

"You're a coward, Billy. If I knew where you lived, I'd come over and shove whatever you're shooting right down your throat."

"Now you're threatening *me?*" His voice rose in pitch. "Nobody threatens me and gets away with it!"

Billy told me his address and the color of his apartment building. Stupid dope head.

"Don't go anywhere," I said. "It'll take me a couple hours to drive over there. You might want to rest up."

Without a word, Billy hung up. I got a new dial tone and dialed 9-1-1. If Billy really thought I was still in Seattle, he might take the opportunity to take a shot at Carla. If he believed I was as close by as I was, the timeline was even shorter.

24

■ Billy's home was a daylight basement apartment in an aging gray house on Englewood Avenue. I had no trouble finding it because the police had beaten me there. They already had three squad cars there, the flashing lights guiding me in like a runway at a small airport.

I parked the Land Cruiser on the street in front of a row of mailboxes and went in search of the officer in charge.

A young cop with a blond buzz cut held up his hand and stopped me before I even set foot on the front lawn. "I'm sorry, sir. We have an emergency situation here. I can't allow you to go beyond this point."

"I know," I told him. "I'm the one who called it in. I know the woman being held in there."

We were both forced to raise our voices in order to be heard. Loud music thumped from the basement apartment, above the legal decibel levels for a residential area. The curtains were drawn on the picture window cut out of the concrete foundation of the house, but the window itself was open, allowing the music to blast free from its confines. The speed metal rhythm, *chugga-chugga-chunk, chugga-chugga-chunk*, made it all but impossible for the police to be heard through their megaphones.

The young officer just shook his head at me, when a sharp *crack* tore through the punching rhythm of the music. Billy's black 4x4 exploded through the door of the garage that was twenty feet away from the main house, made a ninety-degree turn, and barreled toward us.

Three cops drew their side arms, but Billy fired first. With his right hand on the steering wheel, Billy leaned out and fired potshots at the police cruisers. I thought I heard the *thunk* of a bullet penetrating sheet metal, but with the blaring music, the roar of Billy's truck and the gunshots, it was hard to tell.

Two cops returned fire immediately. At least one of them missed their target, and the picture window of Billy's apartment shattered and fell like a cascade of diamonds in the sunlight while I leapt out of the path of the fleeing truck and flying bullets.

Billy hit the street doing about forty and made a screeching hard left. In the span of two breaths, the cops all piled into their black and whites and raced off in a blare of sirens and tire smoke in pursuit of their prey.

I was last, making a sharp U-turn on Englewood and gunning it to keep up with the chase. Billy had turned right on 40th, and then headed east on Lincoln Avenue a block later. I popped on my emergency flashers and kept my foot on the gas until I was only a few yards behind the last police car.

Ahead of the pack, Billy weaved through the cars that had delayed getting out of the way. With three cop cars, sirens screaming, lights flashing, coming up fast in their rearview mirrors, it surprised me how slow people were to move to the side of the street, or at all, in order to let them pass.

Telephone poles whipped by so fast, they looked like they'd merged into one long brown picket fence. People in their yards glanced up with open mouths and houses blurred into one long multicolored structure. We burned by a school and a church on the way up a slope. I had no idea what was on the other side and let up on the gas just enough to keep control if the Land Cruiser caught some air. The hill wasn't steep enough for that, but at the top, I glimpsed a Christmas tree of swirling blue and red lights at an intersection less than a mile away — a roadblock.

A *pop*, like an exploding balloon, brought my attention back to the pursuit in front of me. The three police cars suddenly fanned out into a staggered position. Another *pop*. I looked forward to the black 4x4 and saw Billy's right hand wrapped around a black pistol, firing at us through the sliding back window.

After two more shots, he pulled his hand back inside the cab, and his taillights lit up. He was less than fifty yards from the roadblock at the intersection. With a squeal from the tires and a wall of blue smoke, the truck swerved left across the oncoming lanes. It bounced up an embankment landscaped with lava-colored bark chips and stringy-leaved yucca plants. At the top, Billy hit a concrete parking bumper and launched the front end of the truck about five feet into the air. When it came down, he lost control, shot across the sparsely populated parking lot, and crashed through the wall of a McDonald's restaurant.

The pursuing cops and I arrived within seconds, each of us screeched to a halt to form a barrier of vehicles along Lincoln Avenue. I saw two black-and-whites pull away from the roadblock and zip around to the back of the restaurant, while the other cops drew their weapons and, from the cover of their own vehicles, trained them on the tailgate of Billy's truck.

I jumped from the Land Cruiser, left the door open, and crept up on the young cop who'd tried to stop me at Billy's apartment.

"You can't be here," he said.

"Yeah, I know. But I'm in the middle of this whole thing. The guy in the truck is Billy somebody and he's doped up, probably on meth. He makes it, too. He also has a hostage, a woman named Carla Caplicki from Seattle who he kidnapped last night."

"Who are you?" the cop asked.

"Ray Gordon. Listen, I had a run-in with this guy and he's nuttier than a Snickers bar. You don't want this to get any uglier than it is."

"By 'run-in,' you mean he did that to your face?"

I touched the bandage over my nose and remembered how the bruises around my eyes had turned the color of an eggplant overnight. I nodded. "Yeah, that's what I mean."

The officer blinked at me, then twisted around to face the other two police cars we'd trailed to the scene. He thumbed the radio transmitter hanging on his shoulder and said, "Hey, Sarge, this is Williams. I got a guy over here with some information on the perp in there. You might want to hear it. Over."

I looked down the short row of cars and saw one of the police officers crane his neck in our direction. It was Sgt. Dade, the same giant cop who had shown me the police record of Walt's death, and I gave him a "yo" kind of wave. He leaned toward his shoulder and said something. From Williams's radio, I heard a tinny, "Roger that."

The Sergeant slowly stood but remained in a crouched posture as he made his way over. Two shots rang out from inside the McDonald's, and Dade ducked behind the tire of one of the police cruisers as the light bar on top shattered from a bullet impact and rained bits of colored plastic all around him.

"This better be worth it, Williams!" Sergeant Dade yelled.

Officer Williams glanced over his shoulder at me. "Don't worry," I said. "It's worth it."

The police weren't about to open fire on Billy. A restaurant full of innocent citizens was not the place to stage a gun battle between a doped-up scumbag and the law. I doubted if Billy knew that, and as if to prove it, one more shot came from inside the McDonald's like an exclamation point to his first two volleys.

"Okay, we got ourselves a shooter," said Sgt. Dade as he landed next to me with his back against the car, "so make it fast. What've you got, Gordon?"

I told the Sergeant exactly what I'd told Officer Williams, but also laid out in detail what had happened at the cabin and the phone calls between Billy and me.

"Tell me again why he clocked you," Sgt. Dade said.

"I looked in his truck. His son was sleeping inside the cab."

"But you didn't touch the truck or threaten the boy?"

"Nope." I shook my head. "But he was ready to tear me a new one, anyway."

"Marvelous. A real jewel of the community."

"Hey, coppers!" Billy yelled from inside the McDonald's. "Are you guys hungry? I'm gonna have a Big Mac before I come out and teach you all a lesson."

Williams and Sgt. Dade looked at each other. Then Billy appeared at the ragged hole in the wall, with an elderly woman who made King Tut's mummy look only one thousand years old instead of three thousand. He had one hand on the woman's bony, sweater-clad shoulder, and held his gun to her head with the other. Where was Carla? I wondered.

"I see you out there, Gordon!" Billy called. "You're hidin' behind your pussy cop friends!" He wore the same fatigues from the day before, and I found myself wondering how long it had been since he'd taken a shower. He ducked behind the broken brick wall and screamed at someone inside, "I don't care what time it is! Just make me a hamburger!"

There was movement inside the cab of Billy's truck. The back window was still open, and I could see Carla struggling to sit up on the seat. She must have been knocked for a loop when they crashed through the wall. She was rubbing her head and I tried to will her to quit moving, to not capture Billy's attention, but it was too late.

"Hey, Gordon," Billy yelled, as he moved next to the truck, the old woman side stepping in front of him, "it looks like your girlfriend is waking up. I'm gonna get to have my fun after all!"

"Do you have any sharpshooters in place, Sarge?" I asked.

"They're on the way," Dade said.

Billy opened the driver's door of the truck and pulled Carla across the seat by her hair. She tried to move quicker, to give him nothing to pull, but she was lethargic, still trying to get her bearings, while Billy was keyed up and impatient. He reached further, grabbed around her neck, and heaved.

Once Carla stood in front of him, Billy shoved the old woman aside. She screamed and fell down to her hands and knees. She struggled to stand, looking like a newborn colt on wobbly legs, but she didn't have the strength and collapsed into a mound of gray hair and baby blue wool.

Officer Williams was on his feet in an instant and moved around the patrol car. "Get your ass back here," Sgt. Dade growled, but Williams kept moving. He held up his left hand and holstered his sidearm with his right. Then, with both palms facing Billy, he walked forward.

"What do you think you're doing, cop?" Billy yelled.

Officer Williams kept walking. "I just want to help the lady, okay?"

With his right hand, Billy kept his gun pointed at Carla while he reached back inside the truck with his left. He pulled out the little boy by the back of his clothes and plopped him on the ground at his feet.

Williams stopped.

"Oh, Christ," Dade muttered next to me.

"I don't remember giving you permission to come over here," Billy said to Williams. "Do you remember me saying you could come over? Jeremy, do you remember what I told you about asking permission?" Billy said it loudly, to make sure we could all hear him preach.

The little boy stared at the police officer, who stood in front of him with his hands raised up, and nodded blankly. "This mean man didn't ask permission," Billy said.

Williams took a half step back, but it was too late.

Billy shot him from ten yards away.

Carla and the old lady screamed. The impact lifted Williams off his feet and knocked him against a minivan in the parking lot. Jeremy flinched at the sound of the shot but continued to stare at the policeman his father had just gunned down.

"Hold your fire!" Sgt. Dade yelled. "Hold your fire!"

"Ha!" Billy screamed and jumped up and down behind Carla. "You see that? Ha! One shot! Let that be a lesson to the rest of you!"

From where I was, I couldn't see all of Officer Williams, but I could see his feet and they weren't moving. If Billy was willing to gun down an unarmed cop, it wouldn't take much for him to kill Carla, the old lady, or whoever had fried his hamburger in the kitchen.

Behind us, in a grocery store parking lot, a dark blue moving van with *Yakima Police* stenciled on the side pulled in and stopped. I patted Sgt. Dade on the shoulder. "I hope those guys are good shots." Then I walked around the car.

25

■ "Hey, fella," Dade said. "Just what do you think you're doing? Get back here or I'll shoot you myself, and then I'll arrest you for obstruction of justice."

I stopped and turned around. "You know my name, Sarge. It's not fella. And I'm not obstructing justice, I'm going to speed it up." I looked past Dade to the SWAT team assembling by the van. "Know what I mean?"

Sgt. Dade shook his head and stood up. I backed away from him. "I'm the one he wants to kill, Sarge. There's no reason to send in more of your guys and then me at the end. Okay?" I didn't wait for an answer. I turned on my heel and started walking.

The distance between Billy and myself was measured by two traffic lanes, a sidewalk, maybe five yards of landscaping, and then three car lengths of black asphalt parking lot. Overall, just a matter of seconds to walk, but when moving toward a man holding a gun, who was willing to kill and wanted to kill *me*, time slowed down to an excruciating crawl.

Einstein's Theory of Relativity said a specific event happened at a speed relative to those who observed it. Or something like that. I hadn't majored in physics, but I knew it was close. Anyway, I'm sure Sgt. Dade thought I moved too fast. I felt like my feet were made of concrete blocks. I didn't give a damn what Billy thought.

I looked at Carla. The left side of her face was bruised, there was a cut at her hairline, and a smudge of blood had dried across her forehead. She never took her gaze off of me. Jeremy, the little boy, was as empty as a piece of white paper. I didn't think my presence even registered.

Billy didn't say anything as I walked toward his position. He nodded like I was doing exactly what he wanted, and kept his pistol pointed at Carla's head. When I reached the minivan in the parking lot, I chanced a look at Officer Williams. A black hole the size of a quarter was between the left breast pocket and middle button of his uniform, but there was no blood. I looked at Williams's face and his eyes blinked open.

I knelt beside him and lightly held my palm against his chest to keep him from getting up.

"Don't touch him!" Billy yelled. "The stupid cop got exactly what he deserved. Now it's your turn, Gordon. Come on."

I stood up and took two more steps, my eyes searching for anything I could use as a weapon or a diversion to let the snipers get a clear shot. "Okay. Here I am. Let her go now."

Billy started to laugh, and I stopped walking.

"What's so funny?" I asked.

"Have you seen your face?" Billy said. "Look at those shiners! One punch is all it took for that." He started laughing again, an idiotic mixture of super-villain giggle and self-righteous bravado.

I expected to hear a gunshot at any moment. While Billy laughed, enjoying himself and his self-motivating accomplishments, he moved enough for a good rifleman to squeeze a shot around Carla. But the shot came from much closer. Instead of a report from on top of the SWAT van in the grocery store parking lot, I heard the roar from right behind me.

Billy yowled like a kicked cat and collapsed onto one knee. Carla jerked away from him, picked up Jeremy, and ran toward me. I was yelling for her to get down when Billy took aim and fired.

Everything happened too fast. I heard gunfire from both sides and I didn't know which way to move.

Billy's shot—*Bang!*—clipped my shoulder and spun me around. I went down in front of the old woman who held her purse over her head for whatever protection it could offer. Two more shots—*bang! bang!*—were fired from behind me. Both rounds hit Billy and he fell backward. I grabbed Carla by the feet and yanked her down.

Billy struggled to stay upright. He stared hard at me when he brought his gun up again with a shaky hand.

Another shot came from further behind, and Billy's head snapped back in a spray of blood, just as he pulled the trigger and blew out the rear driver's side tire of his truck. He collapsed with his feet beneath him, so it looked as if he didn't have the rest of his legs below the knees.

His drug-riddled body, like a pile of sticks held together by baggy clothes, lay crumpled over the rubble of the ruined wall.

The police swarmed the scene and guided ambulance crews through the rubble, so they could deliver aid to Williams, Carla, the elderly woman, and me. Sgt. Dade hunched down next to Williams, helping him remove the bulletproof vest that had saved his life. The old woman complained of a bad hip, scuffed knees, and how it was a good thing she was already deaf with all the gunfire going on. Carla's hands shook as she helped me sit up against Billy's black 4x4. She fussed over the bloody tear in my arm.

"Just a scratch," I told her.

"I'm sorry, Ray."

"For what? Carla, you didn't do anything wrong here."

"I should have seen him coming. I should have fought him more," she whispered.

"Carla—" I scooted closer to her "—don't think that. This is not your fault. If anyone is to blame, it's me. Okay? I got this hot head riled up, not you."

She nodded, and I put my good arm around her. She leaned closer. "Ouch," I said, and Carla burst into tears.

"Well, Ray Gordon. What have you got to say for yourself?"

I looked up and saw Sgt. Dade towering above me, his arms crossed like a knot of tree limbs. "How about I'm sure glad I had your fine policemen here to save my life today," I said.

"That'll do for now. Let the EMTs fix you up. Then one of my officers will bring you to the station, and you can tell me just what the hell this is all about. Understood?"

"Yes, sir."

26

■ Carla and I were given a ride to the Yakima Police station and escorted to an interrogation room. It was carpeted and had padded chairs, so it must have been more of a Q&A room for friends and families rather than criminals and suspects.

My left bicep was cuffed with a bandage. It felt like I was having my blood pressure constantly monitored. Carla had said nothing since an EMT swabbed and put a bandage over the cut on her forehead. I could only wonder what Billy had done to her. We sat in silence across from each other at one end of the table. I studied the wood grain patterns on the surface until the door opened.

Sgt. Dade walked crisply into the room, wearing a clean uniform. He was followed by a man in a blue blazer, white shirt, and red tie. Dade sat at the end of the table closest to Carla and me, placing a folder in front of him. The plainclothesman, whom I hadn't seen at the McDonald's, sat at the head.

"How are you doing, Miss Caplicki?" Dade asked.

"I'm doing fine, thank you," she said quietly.

"We have counselors if you'd like to talk to someone about what happened."

The guy at the other end of the table nodded and glanced at Dade, then back to Carla. He didn't look like a counselor to me, but then Sgt. Dade looked more like a brick wall than a cop.

Carla started to say something, but stopped. She folded her hands on the table and lowered her eyes.

"What is it, Carla?" I asked.

She looked at me, then to the man at the end of the table before turning to Sgt. Dade. "It's just that…I'm glad the little bastard is dead. I'm sorry."

Dade's face cracked into a smile. "I think you'll be fine. Believe me, you're not the first person to have a gun pointed at her head, end up in a gun battle, and then be happy the cause of it all wound up dead." He patted her hand. "Don't feel sorry for being a survivor. Now, Mr. Gordon—" he swiveled his chair in my direction "—speaking of *causes*."

Not exactly what I'd call a masterful segue, but Dade was a giant cop, not a literary giant. Clichés aside, I wasn't ready to lay it all out on the table without first knowing how Williams was doing.

"He's all right," Dade said. "He's up at the hospital getting looked at, but word is he'll be fine."

"What about Jeremy?" Carla asked.

Dade sighed. "We know his mother. She's been locked up on prostitution charges. She confirmed Billy is the father. That kid's going to have a tough life. The doc says he was probably born addicted to meth."

Carla shook her head and looked at the ceiling as her eyes got moist.

Sgt. Dade then opened the folder in front of him and paraphrased his report of the incident for us. I greatly appreciated this, since he was under no obligation to share his report. He brushed past the standoff at Billy's apartment, waving his hand at it with a sour look on his face. Obviously, he was miffed about Billy being in the garage and not in the apartment.

He skipped the high-speed chase as well, glancing up at the man in the blue blazer as he did. With hot police pursuits in the news every week, I figured it was a point of contention between the two men and best left to office politics.

Sgt. Dade picked up the story in earnest when Officer Eric Williams was shot at close range with a 9mm round fired by the perpetrator, one Billy Bradley. Williams suffered severe bruising and probably a broken rib, but doctors had yet to confirm the latter. There was no speculation, however, that the mandatory bulletproof vest worn by Officer Williams had saved his life.

When I had approached Billy, Williams had been of the same mind as me: shoot the bad guy, save the girl. Williams, from the ground, put a bullet through Billy's right ankle and turned it into nothing more than a few splinters and chunks of worthless calcium.

No longer able to bear his own weight, Billy had collapsed and taken two more shots to the upper body from Williams's gun. Either the massive amounts of methamphetamine in his system, or his extreme hatred for me (as illogical as it was) kept him upright.

The final shot, a bullet that carved a tunnel through Billy's thick, single-minded skull, had come from a sniper's rifle.

Sgt. Dade closed the folder and looked at me. "Now, Ray, how about you tell us why all of this happened. Can you do that?"

I began with Walter Kelly's death and related to Dade everything that had happened over the last few days. Since breaking and entering was a crime, I left out the snooping I'd done inside Brian Kelly's house, but I did include my suspicions about the veterinarian, his pharmacist wife, and the family squabble about the cabin west of Rimrock Lake.

"Are you sure they're cooking meth up there?" Dade asked.

I nodded. "Ninety-nine percent sure. I didn't see inside, but all the junk in the back and the nasty smell point to meth."

"What did it smell like?"

"It was strong, like super ammonia or something. It burned my nose more than anything."

Dade and the mystery man stared at one another and a knowing look passed between them.

"I believe everything you've told us, except for the finger pointing at Brian Kelly." Dade leaned back in his chair.

"Why?" I asked.

"Because I've known Brian for a long time. He's even the vet for my dog. Now I don't know anything about a family cabin, but I do know illegal drug trafficking is not what Brian and Julie are all about. They've got a six-year-old little girl, for Christ's sake."

"Which means diddly," Carla said.

"I'm sorry?" said Sgt. Dade.

"How can you say that after what happened today? Obviously having a child is not a deterrent for parents who make or sell drugs. It's in the paper every day and nobody does anything about it."

"Miss Caplicki—" Dade's voice rose like a teacher not about to be smart assed by a child, "—I hardly think—"

"All right, that's enough," the man in the blue blazer said. Carla and I both turned to stare at the man we forgot was even there. "I think we're done here," he said. "Sergeant, alert the Health Department about the cabin. Let them know we're going up to take a look within the hour. I'll get a search warrant issued inside twenty minutes. Then assemble an assault team. Mountain terrain is not our normal turf. Make sure they're prepared for anything. Understood?"

"Yes, sir," Dade said. "What about the sheriff?"

"I'll let them know what we're up to, but this fell into our laps. I want everything related to be handled by us, as well."

Dade nodded. Both men stood up and started to walk for the door while Carla and I just sat there, stunned to hear someone give orders to Sgt. Dade.

The man in the blue blazer stopped. "I hope we can count on you for your continued cooperation, Mr. Gordon."

"Of course."

"Good. I'll need you to guide Sgt. Dade and his men to the cabin."

"Absolutely," I said.

He nodded curtly and followed Dade out the door.

"That guy leads two lives," Carla said. "By day, he's a cop. By night, he's Batman."

"What? Why would you say that?"

"Strong silent type. Like the guy who's Batman."

"You don't even know Batman's real name?"

Carla shrugged. "I don't know this guy's name, either."

27

■ Going back to the Kelly family cabin surrounded by a posse of gung-ho cops didn't really convey a summer picnic atmosphere, but I thought Walter would approve. His cabin, a labor of love for him and his two buddies, was being used as an illegal drug factory. Even if it turned out Sgt. Dade was right and I was wrong about Brian Kelly, someone was trespassing, and if that was all they got busted for, they'd be lucky.

I rode in the passenger seat of a black and white Ford Explorer, with *Yakima Police* splashed on the sides in red-and-blue decals and a matching neon-colored light bar mounted on top of the cab. Sgt. Dade drove, and another officer sat in the rear passenger's seat next to Carla.

Carla had insisted on coming along even though she'd admitted to not knowing the location of the cabin or ever having been there. Sgt. Dade had argued that it might be dangerous and he wasn't interested in unnecessarily saving her life a second time in the same day.

"That's a load of bullcrapaloni," Carla had said and climbed into the backseat of the SUV.

I quietly suggested Carla probably wasn't ready to be alone. Dade shook his head, looking up into the sky, as if asking, why me? The officer who sat next to her was then assigned to keep her "secure."

Behind us was an unmarked, white Chevy Suburban which had tinted windows so dark they'd land a private citizen a citation. The Suburban was loaded with six additional officers and an array of weaponry.

Last in line was a small, white car that had caught up to us as we left the Yakima city limits. Judging from the state insignia on the doors, we presumed it was someone from the Health Department.

Just after Naches, we turned south on Highway 12 and started on the winding road into the mountains. We drove by the Chinook Elk Feeding Station, and when I craned my neck, I saw hundreds of elk roaming inside a fenced field.

"What's that all about?" I asked Dade.

"There are too many elk in this area for them all to find food through the winter, so the—"

"Oh, crap!" I said. "Morphy! I forgot all about Morphy!"

"Jesus!" Sgt. Dade said. "Don't do that! I thought I was going to hit something. Who's Morphy?"

"My dog."

"What?"

"He's at the motel. He needs to be fed and walked. Carla, do you have your phone on you?"

"Sorry," she said. "Billy the Scumbag tossed it in his trash before we left."

"Sarge?" I said.

"I don't think so," Dade said.

"Come on. You have a dog. You wouldn't want him locked up in a strange motel room with no food, would you?"

Sgt. Dade sighed and shook his head. "Make it quick." He took his phone from its belt clip and handed it to me.

"I never took you for a softie, Sarge," the officer in the backseat said.

"You can stow that crap right now, Hammond!" Dade glared into the rearview mirror.

I glanced over my shoulder as I put the phone to my ear. Officer Hammond put his arm across his mouth and struggled to keep a straight face.

When our caravan of official vehicles turned off of the main highway and began the bumpy trek to Walter Kelly's cabin, it was a quarter after six and raining. In the city, rain wasn't a problem. There were plenty of lights, drainage pipes, and places to pull over if need be. The road we followed, however, was barely wide enough for one vehicle. The sky was blacker than Billy Bradley's soul, and the rain fell hard enough to make it look like we were driving through a car wash.

Dade shoved the SUV into four-wheel drive and took some pressure off of the gas pedal. Viscous mud squished under the tires and painted the roadside weeds chocolate as we moved further into the forest. October snow certainly wasn't unheard of up in the Cascades, but though it was cold, I didn't believe we were high enough for the white stuff.

The blackness outside turned the side windows into mirrors, so all eyes were on the road ahead, where the headlights illuminated the streaks of rain. Although everyone stared into his or her own world, thinking private thoughts, I hoped Sgt. Dade's thoughts concerned the best way to navigate these water-filled ruts the U.S. Forest Service called a road.

"Did you check out the rest of the chessboard?" Carla asked.

I twisted myself around and looked at her. "Yeah, I did. Nothing else."

"Well," she said with a faint smile, "at least you got the one, right?"

"Right."

"Just what are you two talking about?" Sgt. Dade asked.

"Brian Kelly's father made me a chessboard before he died. Wonder Woman back there found a secret compartment in the board that Walt had put an old photo of my mom in."

"And what does that all mean?"

"Watch the road!" I yelled. Instinctively, Sgt. Dade tapped the brakes and slowed us down before we went over the edge. "This corner is very sharp," I said.

The three cars eased around the near ninety-degree bend and then formed a line across the front of the driveway leading down to Walt's cabin. As we came to a stop, I noticed the thin chain and the biohazard sign I'd smashed through were gone.

Officer Hammond opened a compartment behind his seat and produced four dark green plastic ponchos. We pulled them over our heads and adjusted the hoods before stepping out of the vehicle and into the icy mountain rain.

The men who had driven up behind us were already out of the Suburban and preparing for battle. One cop had his rifle trained on the cabin and looked through a sighting scope. He leaned across the hood of the Chevy while another officer stood beside him and surveyed the area through binoculars. The rest of the troop was on the other side of the Suburban, getting the equipment and weapons ready.

Beyond the SWAT team was the little white car with the State Health Department logo on the doors. Through the rain and gloom, it looked like a giant pile of mashed potatoes. I squinted and focused, realizing how hungry I was. The driver's door opened, and in the greenish glow of the dashboard lights, I recognized him as Margie Kelly's next door neighbor, Ed Carter.

I tiptoed and hopped around several mud puddles to shake his hand. "Ed, I didn't know you were a field man," I said.

He'd donned a bright yellow slicker that made him look like he belonged on a box of frozen fish sticks.

"I'm not, usually." He wiped rain off of his brow. "But when I heard who owned the property, I thought I should be the one to come out and take a look. What are you doing here?"

"You could say I had a run-in with the creeps who've been using this place."

He nodded and looked past me. I turned around and saw Sgt. Dade waving us over.

"Night vision hasn't picked anything up," Dade said as we melted into the semi-circle of cops in front of him, "but that does not mean we can relax. With the infrared unit down, we can't be sure no one is inside."

There was a round of chuckling from the police officers at the mention of the infrared unit, and I looked quizzically at Ed for help. He leaned toward me and said, "City budget. There *is* no infrared unit. The city can't pay for one, or won't. Inside joke."

I nodded and listened to Dade finish his instructions. His men were to fan out and take up positions in a U shape around the front of the cabin. Sgt. Dade and the remaining officer would approach the cabin and determine if anyone was inside. If it was clear, Ed could go down, verify a meth lab, and initiate hazardous area clean-up procedures.

Everyone nodded, and Carla and I caught each other's eye. I ducked through the dispersing cops and stood next to her.

"You okay?" I asked.

"Getting better by the minute, although I could use a big fat bacon cheeseburger."

"Red Mill—" I nodded "—with fries and a vanilla shake."

"As cold and wet as I am right now, I think I'd make mine a hot cocoa."

"Sacrilege, Miss Caplicki." I draped an arm around her. "I don't think I could be seen with someone who didn't eat a Red Mill hamburger properly."

"That's okay," Carla said. "I think Officer Hammond has his eye on me."

"That's because he's guarding you."

She elbowed me.

In the near distance, I watched the disc of Sgt. Dade's flashlight float up the front door of the cabin to where a gleam of metal revealed the padlock I'd seen the day before. Dade knocked on the door. There was no response, so he and the other officer disappeared around the side. When they emerged unscathed from the other side, Dade waved to Ed Carter.

I pushed off the police 4x4 where I was leaning and walked around to join Ed. Carla started to follow, but Hammond put a hand on her shoulder. I shrugged and smiled at her, then trotted down the driveway to catch up to Ed.

"Can you smell anything?" Ed looked at me.

"Yeah. It hurts my nose," I said.

"It's called anhydrous ammonia," Ed said. "They use it to separate the ingredients in the over-the-counter drugs they get. Anhydrous is an agricultural fertilizer. Nasty stuff."

"See all the garbage around back?" I asked Sgt. Dade as I approached him.

He nodded and looked beyond me. "Hey, Carter!" he yelled above the pounding rain. "Can you move it along before we all get washed out into the lake?"

Ed had stopped about twenty feet back. He fiddled with the cell phone in the palm of his hand. "Hold on," he called. "I need to contact the office and let them know we have an active site. I can't dial and walk at the same time."

When I looked back toward Sgt. Dade, it appeared as though someone inside the cabin had turned on the lights. The windows were all illuminated, even those covered by the Seahawks blankets. In the next instant, the tiny building exploded.

28

As chunks of wood, twisted sheets of metal roofing, bits of glass and plastic, and random household items fell around us, I pushed myself up into a sitting position. The blast from the cabin had knocked Sgt. Dade and myself to the ground. I was just checking to see if my arms and legs were still attached when Carla reached me.

She knelt down next to me in the wet grass. "Ray, are you okay?"

"Yeah. Everything's still attached. How about you? Were you far enough back?"

"The car shook like it was an earthquake, but we're fine. What happened?"

I looked at Sgt. Dade. "The fumes and chemicals from meth production wouldn't have done that, would they?" I asked.

"Sure they would," Dade said. He sat up with his arms resting on his knees. His poncho started to collect rainwater like a canvas tent. "The propane and anhydrous ammonia these people use are under pressure. Given the right circumstances, you bet they'd light up like that. Some meth cooks use hot plates, which are safer, but up here with no electricity, they were probably using open flame propane burners. Mix the chemicals and fumes with that, and…" He shrugged.

"And what?"

"Boom." Dade spread his arms out like a ball.

"Kind of convenient it went boom when we got here," I said.

"True," Dade said, "but this stuff is so volatile, anything could set it off."

The officer with the binoculars marched up to our impromptu huddle and asked if any of us were in need of medical attention. Dade shook his head. "We're all right, Jonesy. Round everyone up. I want a head count to make sure we're all still alive before we do a canvas of the area."

Jonesy trotted back up toward the Chevy Suburban he'd arrived in. I followed his slippery progress until my gaze fell on a bright yellow rain slicker lying in the clearing at about the same spot I'd wandered across Billy's pickup truck.

"What happened to Ed?" I asked and stood up.

Carla and Sgt. Dade stood up as well and looked around in the darkness. "He wasn't *that* close to the cabin," Carla said.

"Anyone see the Health Department guy?" Dade yelled.

Jonesy was by the three vehicles at the top of the driveway and he turned his flashlight toward the small white car Ed had driven up in. "He's up here, Sarge," Jonesy called. "He's in his car."

Ed Carter sat behind the wheel of his car with his hands in his lap and his eyes unblinkingly forward. His hair was plastered to his skull by the rain and water dripped from the curled up ends at his neck. Sgt. Dade opened the door and shined his flashlight on the steering wheel.

"Ed, you look a little stunned," I said, hunching down so I was level with him. "Did you get hurt? Are you okay?"

"I have some vacation time coming," Ed said. "I think I'll go someplace warm."

His eyes never moved, his voice was soft, as if he was consoling a child. I didn't see any blood or any other evidence that he was injured.

"Ed, how about you let one of the police officers take a look at you?" I said.

He shook his head slowly. "I'm on vacation as of right now."

Ed reached past me and closed the door. I had just enough time to stand up and step back before it shut. He turned over the engine and rolled down the window. "Nice to have met you folks, but I'm outta here."

"Hold on one second," Sgt. Dade said. "What are you going to do about this?" He waved his flashlight toward the burning rubble that was once Walt Kelly's cabin.

"Don't worry," Ed said. "I'll let the people who need to know, know."

"Tonight?" Dade asked.

"I work for the government," Ed said. "You're lucky *I* came out this late."

"Why did you, then?"

"It was personal. Don't worry. A crew will be here tomorrow morning."

Ed dropped the shift lever into reverse and backed the tiny car up about ten yards before turning the wheel and sending the rear tires up the side of the hill. He made a tight three-point turn, then disappeared around the sharp corner on his way down the mountain.

"Personal?" Dade looked at me. "What was that supposed to mean?"

"He was Walt Kelly's neighbor," I told him.

29

The next morning, I examined my face in the motel room mirror and found several small cuts. I didn't remember getting hit by debris from the cabin explosion, but everything had happened so fast.

It didn't matter. Combined with the broken nose and black eyes, my face looked more and more like a kindergartner's papier-mâché art project. Carla would be sympathetic, but only until she remembered we had only a few hours before her friend's wedding.

Morphy was on the bed watching television when someone knocked on the door. He barked once then turned his attention back to the morning news. When I opened the door, I wasn't surprised to see Carla standing there.

We'd gotten back to the motel around eleven p.m. I'd offered to give her the bed in my room, even promised that Morphy and I would sleep together in the other one, but Carla had insisted on getting her own room. I suspected it might have had something to do with rebuilding the courage to be alone again after something that traumatic, but I hadn't asked. After she'd booked a room, we'd gone in search of something to eat.

Red Mill was a Seattle establishment, which meant we'd had to find something else. Neither of us had suggested McDonald's for obvious reasons, and pizza seemed iffy at best, since I'd never got a straight answer from the Kellys. We'd settled on a fairly nice restaurant that was willing to serve us dinner at such a late hour, and had slid into a booth seat by the window.

After a couple of hours in cold mountain rain and mud, coupled with a meth-lab explosion, Carla and I had looked like we'd just come from the set of a disaster film. But neither of us were famous, the wet was real, the fatigue weighed heavily, the cuts bled, and the bruises were sore. People had stared. We'd smiled back. And when dinner came, we'd devoured it without ever saying a word to each other.

Standing before me the next morning, Carla's hair was damp from a shower and she'd tried unsuccessfully to cover her bruises with make-up. The result was a doppelganger in mid-transformation.

"Breakfast?" I asked.

"I'm still stuffed from last night. I'll watch you eat."

We walked a couple of blocks until we found a diner, where I ordered fried ham, eggs, and hash browns. Carla wanted coffee. The waitress brought us two cups, though it wasn't as good as we would have found in Seattle. We doctored it with sugar and cream.

"We're going to be quite a pair at the wedding," Carla said.

"What wedding?"

"You're drinking the next cup black," she said.

"Oh. *That* wedding." I smiled. "We could skip it."

"Ray, I was asked to play an important role in the wedding. I can't just not go."

"Looking like that? Do you think what's-her-name will still want you in all her pictures?"

"Oh, God. Is it that bad?"

I chuckled. "Just wishful thinking on my part. Don't worry. People will just think we had a killer party the night before."

"Which was last night," Carla said. "You still don't have your tux, now do you?"

"Nope. We'll have just enough time to breeze into town, pick it up, and then on to the wedding. Sgt. Dade said we could head back today, and he'd call if he needs any kind of statement."

"But that won't be the end of it, will it?"

I shook my head. Carla already knew my theory. That guy didn't just happen to come across Walt's cabin by accident. Someone, probably Brian Kelly, had told him it wasn't being used and never would be. "You know what, though," I said. "Walter found out."

"What do you mean?" Carla asked.

"Somehow Walter found out that his cabin was being used, and so they killed him. I thought Brian killed him so he could sell the place, but when you think about it, keeping it as a meth lab would make him a lot more money."

"I thought his death was an accident," Carla said.

I shook my head. "I don't believe it for a second. Not anymore."

Carla pulled my plate in front of her and scooped up a forkful of hash browns. "Mmm. These are good."

"The ham was excellent. Are you trying to change the subject?"

"Me? No, I've always thought bad coffee with discussions about drug dealers and murder is a great way to start off the morning."

"Okay. What do you want to talk about?"

"How long did it take for you to try out your new chessboard?" She smiled and ate another forkful of hash browns.

"I thought you weren't hungry."

The chessboard wasn't something I really wanted to talk about. Maybe if I hadn't been so embarrassed by my reaction to the photograph, that night might have turned out differently. Maybe Carla and I would have finally gotten cozy, and Billy wouldn't have been able to hurt her.

"Don't change the subject," she said.

"I think it was about six point seven seconds after you closed the door," I said.

"And?"

I made a face like I wasn't happy with a choice of curtains. "I need some different chess pieces."

"Of course you do."

"None of mine do it justice. Walt's chessboard is a work of art. It deserves the same."

"And I bet you already have some in mind, don't you?"

"House of Staunton Collector series in ebony with a four-point-four-inch King and fitted case." I gave her a knowing nod like a salesman who shows only top-of-the-line merchandise.

"Oh, my. Sounds spectacular. And what did you play? Did you play your correspondence games?"

"Nope. I played through the Evergreen Game. Walt called me about it last week before we were supposed to have our lesson. He said he was having a problem with it."

"How in the world did you manage with sub-par pieces?"

I squinted at her. "You're developing a very sarcastic tongue, Miss Caplicki. I think I like it."

She grinned and scooped the remaining hash browns into her mouth. "What's the plan for this morning?"

"I need a new cell phone. I say we head to the mall, then get Morphy, check out, and go home."

We strolled back to the motel to retrieve my car and headed for the one mall in Yakima. The drive was a straight shot down 1st Avenue, but involved about seventeen traffic lights, all of which were red, which turned the trip into a half-hour of stop and go.

The mall was a long spread-out affair on one level. We spied a number of senior citizens doing laps around the corridor. After sidestepping a bevy of old ladies, Carla and I found a store for my cell phone company.

I dropped a handful of plastic bits and shards of green circuit boards on the counter—what was left of my phone—and the young lady who was helping me suddenly understood my predicament. She showed me a number of phones, some the size of a Hot Wheels toy car and some larger models, and we discussed an array of accessories and options. In no time, I was reconnected with the world thanks to modern technology.

"Wow," Carla said as we walked out of the mall, "New chessboard, new phone. What's next?"

"Maybe a new girlfriend," I said.

"Oh? I wasn't aware you had an old one."

With a heart-palpitating realization that my mouth had just acted without consulting my brain, I took several silent steps while thinking of what to say. Why I'd mentioned a girlfriend to Carla, I really didn't know. With both of us looking beat-up, and in the middle of a traumatic week, it wasn't the best time to discuss taking our friendship to the next level. "Well, you know…" I tried.

Pathetic.

Just then, my new cell phone rang and I silently thanked God with a brief look up to the clouds. I flipped open the phone. "Hello?"

"Ray, it's Sgt. Dade from the Yakima Police Department. I'm glad you got your new phone so quick."

"Me too." I glanced at Carla.

"Listen, we found the Health Department guy's phone last night, but I don't remember his name."

"It's Ed Carter, Sarge. I'm going that direction. Do you want me to drop it off?"

"Would you? That'd be great."

On the way to the police station, Carla and I laughed about how Dade had made it a point to give me directions to the mall after I'd borrowed his phone the night before. Luckily, the girlfriend subject never came back up.

Sgt. Dade met us in the lobby of the police station and handed me Ed's phone. "This Carter fella looked pretty shook up last night. If he's home, make sure he's okay, will you? He might have a concussion or gotten hit by something. Since he didn't let us check him out, I want to make sure."

I nodded. "Of course. Were you able to figure out what happened with the explosion? I still find it hard to believe the place just happened to blow up when we were about to go in."

"Plastique," Dade said. "It was rigged. My guess is photo-electric sensors placed somewhere in the woods. I got a forensic team up there now doing a more thorough search of the area."

"Sounds good. We're heading back to Seattle. You have my number if you need anything." We shook hands. Dade told Carla to take care of herself, and then disappeared through a door.

Carla and I went outside and got in my Land Cruiser. "Plastic explosives don't sound small time," she said. "Not that I know anything about them, but they're always a big deal in the movies."

"No, it's not small time." I turned over the engine. "Which makes me even more certain Billy wasn't alone. A burn-out like him doesn't strike me as techno-savvy enough to wire a bomb without blowing himself up."

"I'd agree with that," Carla whispered.

I looked over at her. She seemed small. Carla had never been one to back down from anything, but she'd been through a lot the last few days, enough to make anyone shrink from the unfamiliar. "Let's go check out of the motel, get Morphy, and go home," I said.

"What about Ed's phone?"

I handed her the small, black flip phone and told her to call the last number dialed. "Ed called his office to report the meth lab last night," I said. "Ask them where they are, and we'll leave it with them."

Carla pressed the buttons and held the receiver to her ear. As I turned on to 1st Street and headed for the motel, she lowered the phone to her lap. "No answer," she said. "It just rings. Not even a recording."

"What's the number?"

She looked at the tiny screen on the phone and pressed a button on the keypad. "This can't be right."

"What?"

"The last number he called has a 2-0-6 area code. All of eastern Washington is 5-0-9. Whoever he called last night, it wasn't his office."

"Maybe given the location of the cabin, he thought the Seattle office should take care of it."

"But that doesn't explain why there's no answer at a government office during business hours, not even an answering machine."

"Good point."

I pulled over to the side of the road. I killed the engine and took Ed's phone from Carla. Many cell phone companies embed a service number into their phones. If the user ever had a question or a problem, all they had to do was hit a button, no matter where they were. It was much better than having to carry around an operations manual. I found the right menu page and pressed the call button. In just a few seconds, I was talking to a cheery young lady named Amber who was probably fresh out of high school and excited to be making minimum wage.

"Hi, my name's Ed Carter," I lied. "I have a question about a number on my phone."

"All right, sir, how can I help you?" Amber asked.

"I don't recognize the last number dialed on my phone," I said. "I've called it, but there's no answer, and I'm trying to figure out why it's on my phone. Is that something you can do?"

"We cannot give out personal names. Only those of businesses and those on your service plan. Do you have the number?"

I rattled it off and waited while she punched it into her computer. "Well, Mr. Carter," she said happily, "I think I can safely give you the name of the individual this number belongs to."

"Great. Is the person on my plan?"

"Oh, yes. It's you."

"What?"

"I have you listed as having two phones with two separate numbers, one of which is the number you just gave me."

"Oh, my other phone. Of course. Well, they say since you never call your own phone, you always forget the number." I chuckled and tried to sound embarrassed.

"Yeah, I've heard that," Amber said. "But since you just called it last night…"

"I guess I did. How many times have I called it?"

"Let's see." I could hear the tapping of her keyboard. "Since it went into service, once. Last night."

I thanked her and broke the connection.

"Well?" Carla asked.

"It was his own phone. He didn't call the Department of Ecology. He called another phone that he owns."

"Maybe he was leaving himself a message," Carla offered.

"But why have two phones with different area codes? And where is it?"

Carla shrugged. "It's weird, but there's no law against it."

I nodded and started the engine. Carla was right, there was no law against having a couple of phones registered in different parts of the state, but why would anyone want to? I felt like something in the whole scenario was eluding me, like the odd (but key) turn of a phrase in a trick question. It was there, but it was just out of my reach.

I pulled the shifter into drive, and was checking my mirrors to ease back into traffic when Carla piped up again. She'd already let go of the strange phone number and wanted to hear more about Walt's chess game. Why was it called the Evergreen? Why did Walt have a problem with it? And how come he didn't just give me the board when it was finished? "If he built the board for you over a year ago," she mused, "it's lucky that he sent it right before he died."

She had a good point. I'd forgotten that Margie told me Walt had actually made the board just a few months into our teacher/student relationship. When did he put the picture of my mother in it and decide to send it to me?

"You know I've heard that some people kind of know when their number is up," Carla said. "For no reason, they pay all of their bills and make sure everything is taken care of. Then the next day, they're dead. If that was the case with Walter, if he just felt he was going to be gone, why would he call you about a problem with the Evergreen Game?"

I stared at the dashboard not seeing the gauges, then out the window without seeing the cars passing by.

"Ray? What's wrong?"

"You're right. Oh, my God, you're right!"

30

■ I cranked the wheel to the left, stepped on the gas and made a squealing U-turn in front of a city bus.

"Ray—" Carla had both hands wrapped around the handle above her door " —where are we going? And why are we in a hurry?"

"Ed Carter. It wasn't Brian Kelly, it was Ed Carter who knew about the cabin."

"The Health Department guy?" Carla asked.

I nodded and swerved around a Honda. "He's the Kellys' next door neighbor."

The more I thought about it, the more sense it made. The biohazard sign in front of the cabin should have been a tip-off, but I had wanted to believe it was Walt's son Brian. "Ed *told* me he was the last person to see Walt alive. He made it a point to tell me that he helped Walt pack my chessboard."

"So?" Carla's focus was trained on the road. Her hands were splayed across the dashboard.

"Ed's second phone. He only called it once the entire time he's owned it, which means he didn't get it for a person, like a daughter or girlfriend, and that one call was last night."

"So?"

"So the cabin blew up a second after he made his phone call. The second phone was the trigger for the plastic explosive."

Carla frowned, and then her eyes went wide. I glanced back at the road and zoomed by a Volkswagen van. "Weren't we just talking about the chess game?" she said.

"*Ed* is why Walt called me about the Evergreen Game. It was a clue. Ed works for the state of Washington, The *Evergreen* State. Walt must have known the jig was up. He called me and said he had a problem with the Evergreen Game. He marked it in his book with *Ed's card*. It was a desperation move. Maybe Ed was blackmailing him or something, I don't know. Walt knew Ed was a drug dealer, and Ed knew Walt was on to him. Neither was going to let the other get away with it, so Ed killed Walt, but not before Walt made his move and called me."

Carla shook her head. "That seems kind of farfetched, Ray. Why not just tell you on the phone, 'I've got a problem with my drug-dealing neighbor'?"

"Probably because Ed was right there in the shop with him at the time. The only thing Walt could think of was the Evergreen Game. Definitely a long shot, but it's not called a desperation move for nothing."

"But why call you? Wouldn't he just call the police?"

I shrugged. "Maybe to protect Margie. If Walt went up to the cabin, he probably saw Billy and thought Ed would sick him on her to keep him quiet."

I stepped on the gas and left some rubber around the right turn onto Tieton Drive. Part of me hoped a patrol car would chase me all the way to Ed Carter's house, but the other part felt he was already gone. Ed had told us the night before he would leave for "someplace warm." He was probably well on his way to Mexico or the Caribbean.

When we turned onto Chestnut Avenue, I slowed down to twenty-five. There was no reason to draw attention to ourselves if Ed was in his house, and a screeching halt would probably cause excessive alarm to Margie Kelly, as well.

I eased the Land Cruiser off the street and into the Kellys' driveway. I pulled up to Walt's wood shop and killed the engine.

"Looks like he's gone," I said with a nod toward Ed Carter's house. There was no car, government or personal, in the driveway. The curtains were all drawn, and the newspaper still lay on the front lawn. "I need to talk to Margie and call Dade. You want to come in?"

"I'll be in, just give me a second. I'm going to go steal his newspaper."

"I'm sure Margie has a paper you can read, Carla."

"Probably, but it's the principle that matters. I'll check his mailbox too. Maybe he got a brochure or something from wherever he went. I'll be Nancy Drew. By the way, hurry up. We have a wedding to get to."

Margie Kelly met me at the back door. She stood inside, wearing a flowery apron and holding a cup of tea. The screen door was still closed and I looked at her through the haze of mesh, my hands in my pockets.

"Good morning, Margie."

"Raymond," she said.

Cold. I'd insulted her family and she was prepared to feud over it.

"Margie—" I shrugged "—I'm sorry for what I said about Brian. It was wrong of me to make accusations. Okay? I know I was wrong, but now I need your help."

"Oh, Raymond." Her face softened as she pushed open the screen door. "What on earth could I help you with?"

I smiled and stepped inside. "Have you seen Ed today?"

Her gaze floated toward the ceiling. "No —" she looked back at me " — I haven't. Odd, isn't it? I usually see him every morning when he goes to work, on account of how early I get up."

"Did he ever go to the cabin with Walt?"

"Oh, sure. They'd always go up a couple of weekends to go fishing, and he came with us once when we took the Davises from across the street."

He'd lied. Ed Carter had flat out lied to me when I asked if he knew where the cabin was. What reason would he have to deny it if he wasn't trying to hide something?

"Ray?" Margie said. "What's going on? Why all these questions about Eddy?"

"Margie, I promise I'll tell you everything." I moved over to her and held her hands in mine. "But right now, my brain's on a one-way street, and time is of the essence, so I'll have to tell you a little later. Okay?"

She nodded.

"Okay. Now, do you have any idea when Walt visited the cabin last?"

Margie reached for her teacup like a child would reach for the comfort of a stuffed bear. Shakily, she brought it to her lips, sipped the steaming liquid, and then she wrapped both hands around the cup. "Two days before his accident."

Bingo, I thought. As I pieced together the puzzle of Walt's death, I found myself staring at the tea-drinking paraphernalia Margie had put out on the counter. Even though it was just her in the house, there was honey in a plastic, bear-shaped squeeze bottle, a sugar bowl with a lid notched for a spoon, and a handful of pink sugar substitute packets like those found in eating establishments. I envisioned the sweet little old lady before me deftly sliding the tiny envelopes into her purse while looking sideways at the waiter while in some ritzy hotel restaurant.

I shook the image from my mind. "Margie, you know what the Internet is, right?"

"Oh, Raymond! I'm old, not stupid. Of course I know what the Internet is. Walter and I just didn't have the need to buy a computer. We'd talked about it, but he would have wanted to put all of his records, bills, taxes, receipts, and everything else he kept in those old gray binders into some silly office program. There was no need, though. Walter was just as meticulous with his bookkeeping as a computer would be. We thought about getting a computer to write letters to friends and my sister, but that's so impersonal."

"Does Brian have a computer you and Walt ever used?" I obviously knew full well there was a computer in Brian Kelly's house.

"Sure," Margie said after another sip of tea. "Walter even used it a few times to buy some things off of that big auction site, eBay."

So Walt had found out someone was using his cabin, and got suspicious after seeing the glass and the propane tanks, and catching a burning whiff of the anhydrous ammonia. Instead of going to the library that night, he'd gone over to Brian's house when they were out (I assumed the parents would have a key to their son and daughter-in-law's house) and conducted some online research. Walt had been surfing the meth sites on his son's computer, not Brian. Once he'd realized what was going on, he'd probably reported it to the local authority on the methamphetamine problem—his next-door neighbor.

I walked over to the kitchen sink and looked out the window. Where was Carla? The Land Cruiser was empty. The newspaper on Ed Carter's lawn was…still on the lawn, but closer to the front porch.

Everything in my field of vision became incredibly sharp and I could hear the whisper of Margie stirring her freshly poured cup of tea. The door to Ed's garage was closed and the light above it was on. The side door facing the driveway, was closed, and the…

There! Movement behind the curtains on the second floor. Ed Carter wasn't gone. He'd come home first, and either Carla had seen him, or his ruptured ego couldn't pass up an opportunity.

"Margie—" I spun around and headed for the back door "—call 9-1-1. Ask for Sgt. Dade and tell him where I am. I'm going next door to Ed Carter's house. Okay? Do you got that?"

"I don't think Ed's home, Ray," Margie said with a confused frown.

"Margie! Call the police. Speak only to Sgt. Dade. Okay?"

I didn't wait for an answer.

31

■ Ed Carter's house was a two-story, white-washed craftsman with a brick foundation. The yard was maintained, but that was all. An elm tree, two stories taller than the house, ballooned over the front walkway and above the street.

Spaced along the foundation masonry of the house were small, three-paned windows. I remembered windows like these from someone's house when I was a kid, and I instantly believed I could fit through. My primary thought was that Ed had Carla upstairs, so if I entered the basement, there would be less of a chance for him to hear me. I never really bothered to think I was an adult male and not a ten-year-old kid playing hide-and-seek.

I ran around the front of the house to the opposite side where a tall cedar fence separated Ed's property from his other neighbor. It drowned the thin strip of frayed lawn in shadow. There were three windows on the main house, two larger ones on the bottom, probably for the living and dining rooms, and a smaller double-hung window on the upper floor. Set back slightly in the brick foundation were two of the small basement windows, one toward the front of the house, the other closer to the backyard. They had both been painted over from the inside with white paint.

I squeezed between the fence and the massive chimney that seemed to divide the place in two and sat down facing the basement window at the rear of the house. With a quick look out into the street, I kicked out the middle pane of glass. Inside, right there, was an old-fashioned, brass swivel lock. I pushed the window open and slid inside. My shoulders wedged against the window casing. I had to back out, then snake myself in at an angle, one arm at a time. So much for being the size of a ten-year old kid, I thought.

A workbench mounted to the wall below the window let me get in without falling all the way to the floor. The surface of the bench was relatively bare, too, which told me Ed Carter wasn't much of a do-it-yourselfer around the house. Once I found my footing on the cement floor, I stood still to let my eyes adjust to the darkness.

Hulking masses took shape in the murky light filtered through the small, paint-covered windows. Against the wall to my right, which was the front of the house, three white ice chests — the big kind drunken fools thought they could fill on deep-sea fishing excursions — were stacked one on top of the other. To my left, near a set of stairs leading up into the house, was a large, open cardboard box full of sandwich-size plastic bags. Maybe Ed brown-bagged his lunch every day, but somehow I thought not.

The bench behind me held a red toolbox, a box of nails, a box of screws, and an extension cord. The toolbox housed a flashlight, which I clicked on. Next, I found six screwdrivers (three flat head, three Philips head) of varying sizes, a claw hammer, and a pair of Vise-Grips.

Then I turned the light at the ice chests. What I saw looked like the set from a horror movie or a police training video. The bottom two coolers were sealed with silver duct tape. Sealed, waterproof boxes of any type, particularly large ones, invited me to think of dead bodies — or more accurately, body *parts*.

The top cooler was not taped shut, and even though there was no odor in the air denoting the presence of rotting flesh, I had to look. The lid opened at about chest height, and I fully expected something inhuman and slimy to leap out the moment I lifted it up. I stood back and used the front edge of the flashlight to lift the plastic lid. Nothing jumped out with claws splayed and screaming bloody murder. Even so, I wasn't prepared for what *was* inside.

Cash. Stacks and stacks of United States currency in several denominations, and bundled into rubber-banded blocks, were piled inside the chest. There had to be at least a hundred grand, if not two.

I lowered the lid and stood still. Somewhere in the house above me, Ed Carter walked. It was faint, like the far-off rumble of a train. I guessed he was still on the upper floor.

Besides the ice chests and the box of plastic baggies, the basement was empty. I walked over to the stairs and placed my foot on the bottom tread. It didn't creak as I slowly put all of my weight on it. Each step, one by one, supported me without broadcasting my presence as I made my way to the top. Ed's house must have been built in the late nineteen thirties to early fifties, and I was pleasantly surprised none of the old boards squeaked.

The door at the top was an old four-panel with a brass plate and knob. It was locked. I flipped a light switch on the wall, and a bare bulb hanging above me plinked on. Lights on the same circuit in the basement went on as well, and I snapped off the flashlight.

Once again, the stairs remained silent while I crept back down to retrieve a slotted screwdriver from the toolbox, but on my second ascent, they woke up.

The fourth step on the way back up to the door creaked like an old man getting out of bed. The sound reverberated throughout the basement. I stopped. There were no immediate sounds or muffled voices from the other parts of the house.

Nothing.

Then the step squeaked again as I lifted my weight off of it and moved up the stairwell.

At the top, I went to work. The door and knob were probably original to the house and I had to really get a good grip before the first screw would turn. There was no point in trying to break the door down. The lock was old, but the landing was only three or four feet square and I wouldn't have been able to get the power behind me.

My only concern was how fast I could take the assembly apart. If Ed had heard the stair squeak, had he ignored it, or was he on alert? Had he harmed Carla, or would he play her as the hostage card?

I had one screw out and was working on the other when I heard something and stopped. My pulse pounded in my ears, but I was sure I heard thumping or something similar, like someone bounding down carpeted stairs. Then it stopped.

Carla must have been giving Ed a fight. Or he knew I was somewhere in his house. I went back to work on the doorknob, twisting the screwdriver too quickly. The blade slid out and scraped the smooth brass plate. I took a deep breath, steadied my hand, and started over more slowly.

Then the lights went out.

32

I was momentarily blinded in the darkness of Ed Carter's basement before my pupils adjusted. I stood up slowly, pressed myself against the wall opposite the light switch, breathed out, and looked at the floor. Gray morning light fanned out beneath the door and illuminated the vinyl flooring at my feet.

No one seemed to be on the other side. Maybe a circuit had blown, or maybe Ed was leaving and had turned off the light from another location. I reached through the dark and touched the hard plastic switch.

Then a shadow moved beneath the door and stopped.

I pulled my hand back and held my breath. Ed knew I was there, but he didn't say anything. He must have heard me fooling with the door, and was wondering in silence if I had gone back down the stairs. It was a standoff, but at least I had the advantage of being able to see his shadow.

Just when I started to wonder how long Ed would stand on the other side of the door, I heard the staccato *click-clack* of a pump-action shotgun.

I crouched as low to the floor and as close to the wall as I could squeeze myself and covered my ears. When he pulled the trigger, the blast tore through the old, wood door and flooded the basement with light, sawdust, and smoke. The concussion knocked me over and I bounced down the stairs like a dropped bowling ball until I hit the floor, sprawled out and deafened, and seeing spots.

The middle of the door was gone, and Ed stared down at me. His face was white, his eyes wide, and through the smoke, he looked determined to be the last person I'd ever see. He pumped a fresh round into the shotgun and took aim, but I rolled into the darkness before he could get the shot off.

Above and behind me, Ed kicked the door. I heard the wood splinter and crack. With a third of it already blown away by the shotgun blast, the rest of it wouldn't last long. While Ed was busy with the door, I got to the bench, grabbed everything on it, and circled back beneath the stairs.

After two more blows, the bottom section of the cellar door broke off its hinge and banged down the stairs. There was too much light to hide in the darkness, so my best chance was to catch Ed off guard. He hadn't come down the stairs yet and I thought he was letting his eyes adjust as I was forced to do earlier. If I could get him to come down just a few steps…

I selected the smallest screwdriver from the toolbox and tossed it across the room. It landed with a clatter on the far side of the workbench. But instead of taking a blind shot at the noise, he fired twice straight down through the landing at the top of the stairs. He'd seen my ploy. A ragged hole opened in the ceiling just in front of me. I shielded my face and jumped back.

Without giving Ed enough time to reload, I jumped up and pulled his leg down through the hole. He spread apart like a track hurdler, the leg I had hold of stretched out, the other one bent at the knee, keeping him from falling into the basement.

"Let go of me!" he yelled.

I replied by jamming his hamstring against the jagged floor timbers.

"Augh! Gordon! You son of a bitch!" he grunted.

I pulled his leg back in an attempt to jab some wood into his thigh muscles, too, but he was a quick learner. The butt of the shotgun slammed into my wounded shoulder and I winced. The force of the blow stunned me, allowing Ed to wrench his leg free of my grip. He lost his shoe in the process, but I twisted around and got both hands on the shotgun before he pulled it back up.

He let go of the gun as I grabbed it, and I lost my balance. With one hand around the grip, my finger was over the trigger and the shotgun went off when I hit the floor. The already big hole in the stairwell landing opened wider.

After three close-range blasts from a shotgun, there was very little area left on the landing to support Ed and he crashed through. I started to roll toward the wall, but gravity won and Ed landed on my legs before I could get out of the way. I heard my ankle crack before the jolt of pain ran up my leg like a crazed electrical current.

Ed kicked me in the face and wrestled the shotgun away from me. I sat up and scooted backward on my hands. He worked the pump of the gun and an empty shell flipped out of the chamber, making a hollow *tink-thunk* when it hit the concrete floor.

"Ed—" I held my hands out "—you don't need to do this. You're a drug dealer and that's one thing. But you don't have to become a murderer."

Ed leveled the gun at me. "Too late, but you're making me work more than Walt did." Then he pulled the trigger.

Click.

I flinched, and Ed pulled the trigger again. Nothing happened. He pumped the shotgun but no shell came out. It was empty. I pulled a screwdriver up off of the floor and threw it at him. The orange plastic handle bounced off his forehead. I grabbed and threw another one, but he ducked.

I forced myself to stand. The last thing I wanted was for him to know he'd injured me. My lip was bleeding, my ankle was either broken or had cracked like a piece of cheap pottery, and I was tired. "We through now?" I asked Ed. "You killed your neighbor, but you didn't get me. Sorry. I think we're done."

"You really messed up a good thing, Gordon. Just where the hell did you come from, anyway? You blow into town one day, to play chess of all things, and just decide to ruin my business. Is that the way it is?"

"Why do you drug dealers think you have a right to conduct a *business* like that?" I asked, flabbergasted. "It's not business, it's predatory and it's criminal."

Ed shook his head. "You think people can make it on a nine-to-five job these days? Everyone needs a little extra cash. Don't be so self-righteous. I simply provided a product I knew was in demand. That's business."

"Tell that to your flunky Billy. I don't know any legitimate company where getting your brains blown out by a sharpshooter is in the office handbook. How did you and he connect, anyway? Was he your cousin or something?"

Ed snorted. "Working where I do, I was able to easily find the most sorry, desperate losers to make the product. He made it and got it for free, I provided the location, lab equipment, and supplies. I had access to files on users so I found them, found their friends. Easy money. Until you decided to stick your nose in and ruin it for me."

"This was about Walt, not you!" I shouted. "I got steered in your direction because you killed him. Did you feel justified in doing that, too?"

Ed shrugged. "I did what I had to do. Same as I'm going to do to you."

He pushed himself up using the shotgun as a crutch. Somewhere above us, still a ways off, we heard the wail of sirens.

"No more ammo, Eddy, and here comes the cavalry."

Ed held the shotgun by the barrel like a baseball bat and came at me with a suicidal war cry.

I ducked and covered my head, but Ed must have known where I was hurt. He swung low and connected with my swollen right ankle. I would gladly have passed out if I didn't truly believe he would bash in my skull with the butt of his gun. If rocks could feel, I think I could sympathize with what it felt like to be crushed into gravel. I lay on the floor like a wrecked car, crumpled and screeching.

Ed cocked his arms, ready to take another swing. I crabbed backward, but I couldn't seem to bring my throbbing ankle down. It remained in the air, in the middle of the strike zone. Just as Ed took a step toward me, my hand fell on the open toolbox. I grabbed the hammer. Using my own body as a lever, I sat up as he swung the shotgun, and my foot dropped down.

Ed missed spectacularly. The momentum twisted him around at the waist, and he lost sight of me. I swung the hammer with everything I had and landed a blow to his kneecap.

If I'd had more leverage, his kneecap might have broken, but I still got the desired reaction. Ed dropped the shotgun and it clattered on the floor. He propped himself against the wall and made low guttural noises like a sobbing gorilla. Spittle shot from his clenched mouth.

I sat up and chucked the hammer to the far side of the basement. "Cops are here, Ed." I panted. "You're done."

"You shouldn't have done that, Gordon," Ed said in bursts of breath. "Never drop your weapon until you know your enemy is dead."

He reached into his pants pocket and pulled out a red and brass shotgun shell, and displayed it to me like a magic coin. He had trouble with his knee as he bent down for the gun. He held that leg back and put his weight on the other bare foot. It gave me the time to lift my hip just enough to slide my hand into my back pocket, then as Ed stood triumphantly, shotgun in hand, I reached out and clamped the Vise-Grips onto his shoeless big toe.

"Drop it, Ed," I said. "If I squeeze these shut, you'll never walk a straight line again."

He smirked as if daring me to do it, and jammed the shotgun shell into the chamber with his thumb. I shook my head and squeezed like my life depended on it.

Ed's toe split under the force of the Vise-Grips, and then popped like a wet radish. He screamed until, mercifully, he passed out and slid to the floor.

A door upstairs crashed open and Sgt. Dade peered through the hole in the stairway floor. "Gordon!" he yelled. "Are you alive down there?"

I gave him a thumbs up. "I'll never eat raw vegetables again, though."

33

■ Carla Caplicki was found upstairs, tied to a chair, with duct tape over her mouth. The paramedics, who patched up the cut on my lip and wrapped my ankle in ice, told me she was okay, otherwise. Very pissed off, but physically unharmed.

They strapped me to a backboard and hauled me up the stairs like a footlocker, and then passed me over the hole in the stairwell landing to Sgt. Dade and his men.

Once outside, the bright blue sky never looked as inviting. I'd never thought of a dark and empty basement as a good place to die, so it was nice to be outside again. It was a different sky than the one I'd seen at Erica Minor's funeral, somehow bluer, maybe a bit crisper, but I was still ready to dive in.

Ed was hauled out behind me by two linebacker-sized cops. Because his hands were cuffed behind him, the cops lifted and moved Ed by his armpits while he hopped as best he could on his good foot. They stood him up several feet away while I was transferred to a gurney.

There was a commotion across the driveway — loud voices and crying. I lifted my head enough to see a flurry of blue cotton and flower print as Margie hurried our way, her elbows pumping like pistons. She jerked to a stop in front of Ed and his sentinels. Margie stared at him, and the two cops looked at each other as if silently asking the other what they should do.

Then as quickly as a cobra strikes at its prey, Margie slapped Ed with all the grief, anger, and frustration she'd stored up since Walt's death. The blow rocked him like a playground tetherball. "Edward Carter!" she screamed. "How could you? How could you do this?"

Ed was bent at the waist, his face turned away. Margie moved to strike again, but one of the female cops on the scene grabbed her arm, turned her around, and led her back to her house.

"Why didn't you guys stop her?" Ed whined. "You can't let her do that to me!"

"Shut up," the cop on his left grumbled and batted Ed on the back of the head.

I closed my eyes and felt the world begin to slip away. There were people around me, police and paramedics, people standing in the street to get a look at what was happening. But I couldn't hear them clearly anymore. Their voices were muffled, as if they were all underwater. As the adrenaline that had kept me moving and alert drained away, it left my ears deaf from close-range shotgun blasts, and my body sore from too many bangs and dings to count.

My limbs were soaked with exhaustion as if they were sponges, and I wanted to sleep. Even the rocking motion, as I was carried over Ed's driveway, seemed to push me closer to the slumbering world.

Then someone squeezed my hand. I opened my eyes and saw Carla looking down at me. Her cheeks were pink where the tape had been ripped away from her skin, but she was smiling.

"I'm sorry about all of this," I said.

"Well, every girl wants a little adventure. But, yeah, this was too much. It's vacation time."

I nodded as best I could and closed my eyes. When I opened them again, I was being loaded into an ambulance. I'd fallen asleep for ten yards. Margie's face hovered above mine and she smiled. "Thank you, Raymond, for setting things right."

"I just wanted to play some chess with Walt," I said. She patted my hand and disappeared.

With a heave from the EMTs and a quick, gut-dropping sensation on my part, I was shoved into the ambulance.

There was a lump on the blanket next to my strapped-in hand that hadn't been there before. "What's this?"

Carla climbed into the ambulance and sat next to me. "They're cookies. Margie left them for you." She held up two plastic bags stuffed with different varieties.

Two bags? I thought. "Morphy!" I blurted. Where was my pal?

"Morphine?" one of the EMTs said. "You're not hurt that bad. You don't need morphine."

"He said, 'Morphy,'" Carla told him. "Morphy's a dog." She patted my chest and said, "Morphy's still at the motel. I'll go get him once you're at the hospital."

"Thanks," I whispered. "You're the best."

"But wait, there's more." She grinned. "You're officially off the hook for the wedding."

"What wedding?"

"Don't make me change my mind."

"Are you sure?" I asked seriously. "I know you wanted to go."

"I'd rather sleep," she said.

"Even better."

"Besides, I don't think they're going to let you out of the hospital in time. But you owe me, mister."

"I hope you're not keeping count."

Carla laughed. "You know my mom used to be a nurse. I think I'll take you over there to recuperate, and she and I can keep an eye on you."

"Sounds good to me." I tried to sit up, but the straps held me down. "Your mom is a babe."

Carla rolled her eyes. "You're lucky you're already hurt. But I'm going to let you have it when you heal up."

"Is that a promise?"

"You know it is." She smiled.

ACKNOWLEDGMENTS

While the writing process itself is generally a singular one, I must thank those who were gracious enough to share their expertise, their knowledge, and their enthusiasm before I sat down at the keyboard. To Mr. Bob Clem, whose friendship is as rich as his skill in the art of woodworking. Lt. Mike Merryman of the Yakima Police Department who took time out of his busy schedule to answer a host of odd, criminal-like questions. And to Inga Wiehl, teacher, editor, and writer extraordinaire, who taught me to always ask for more from my own writing.

Of course credit must be given where it's due. The expert analysis of The Evergreen Game in this novel has been re-worded and paraphrased from *Winning Chess Tactics* (1995, Microsoft Press) by GM Yasser Seirawan with Jeremy Silman.

Finally, thanks to my mom and dad who brought me a life of imagination and adventure by encouraging my love of books

Evergreen Game - 1852
Adolf Anderssen - Jean Dufresne

WHITE	BLACK
1. e4	e5
2. Nf3	Nc6
3. Bc4	Bc5
4. b4	Bb4
5. c3	Ba5
6. d4	ed4
7. O-O	d3
8. Qb3	Qf6
9. e5	Qg6
10. Re1	Nge7
11. Ba3	b5
12. Qb5	Rb8
13. Qa4	Bb6
14. Nbd2	Bb7
15. Ne4	Qf5
16. Bd3	Qh5
17. Nf6	gf6
18. ef6	Rg8
19. Rad1	Qf3
20. Re7	Ne7
21. Qd7	Kd7
22. Bf5	Ke8
23. Bd7	Kf8
24. Be7#	